UNLOCK THE ANGEL

CALLA ZAE

PROSE & CONCEPTS

UNLOCK THE ANGEL

Seraphim Angel Order 1

CALLA ZAE

COPYRIGHT

Unlock the Angel

Copyright © 2021 by Calla Zae

Cover Art Copyright: Calla Zae

Prose & Concepts LLC

210 Park Avenue, Suite #280

Worcester, MA 01609

www.proseandconcepts.com

Library of Congress Cataloging-in-Publication Data

Library of Congress Control Number: 2021944002

First edition Ebook ISBN: 978-1-952820-22-9

First edition Paperback ISBN: 978-1-952820-21-2

For those who who believe in a Forever Love.

.

.

.

"Do not forget to entertain strangers, for by so doing some people have entertained angels without knowing it."

—Hebrews 13:2

ONE

Cathy Lu hammered a nail into the plank of wood on her back deck and thought about her ex-boyfriend—specifically his family jewels. How would he feel if she pounded him like this nail? Yes, it was a morbid thought, but as an ex-girlfriend who had been betrayed, she had every right to feel that way. Cheaters deserved a painful punishment, didn't they? They had to feel all the pain they'd bestowed on their significant other. That should be a law. So, she envisioned all the things that made her feel better. Wasn't that part of the healing process?

She pounded another nail into the wood and admired her work. She'd learned a few handy things during her two-year relationship with Gavin. He had promised to renovate her deck and the new studio she was adding to her house. But promises from a cheating man rusted over time. It made her wary of men's promises in general. Now, she depended on herself.

Cathy had kicked Gavin out of her home four months ago when she discovered several text messages and emails he'd been sending to two other women. She should have suspected something was up when he came home later than usual or when he had unexpected phone calls that took him into another room. She had been too trusting.

She considered herself an intelligent woman, but when she discovered the truth about Gavin, it made her feel stupid. Love had a way of distorting things, and she couldn't afford another loss like that. She was careful now. She had to be. Her heart had shattered, and she had hammered it back together. She sighed at the symbolism of hurting Gavin and also piecing herself together by hammering a single nail. Maybe that idea could make its way into her new greeting card collection.

Despite it all, she had moved on, mending herself one step at a time. Time spent alone gave her the retrospection and the clarity to focus on her company, Luminous Press. She had a small team of people who worked for her, making sure her journals, novelty books, greeting cards, and other miscellaneous products were delivered on time to their vendors. She and her mother, Celia, had started the company eight years ago, when she was twenty-five years old. Working with her mom had taught her how to be a successful businesswoman and a decent person who looked at things with compassion.

Be gentle to everyone. You never know what someone is going through. You can't measure someone else's pain from a personal scale.

Everything was different when it was personal, wasn't it? The measuring scale changed when you were the one experiencing the pain. It was all perspective. No one could ever understand that misery until they'd experienced it themselves. Standing on the outside made it difficult to see the storm from within.

Her mother's wise words echoed in her mind. If only her

mom were still alive, she'd comfort Cathy, reminding her that not all men were the same.

Victor Perez knocked on the glass panel of her sliding door, opened it, and stepped out to the deck. "I'm all done for the day, Cathy. The two bathrooms, kitchen, and living room are all spotless now." He smiled and removed the apron, folding it into his hand.

Cathy rose to her feet and stretched her back. She appreciated his gesture even though she knew that his wife, Rosa, needed him more. Rosa and Victor had been cleaning Cathy's house for the last two years until she fell sick with a thyroid disorder that had gotten worse in the last few months. They had planned on early retirement, but life threw a curveball at them that readjusted their plans. So now, it was just Victor supporting his family. Their daughter, Lizzi, who was also Cathy's friend, lived in New York. She'd come home to visit and assist them whenever she could.

"Do you need me to help you with anything else before I head home?" Victor asked.

The weight of his wife's illness sagged on his face even with that adorable smile. The eyes and facial features revealed a lot of things that people didn't realize.

Cathy tapped the hammer against her hand. "I've got it handled. Thank you, though. Please send my best to Rosa. How's she doing?"

Victor sighed, and his shoulders drooped. "She's improving slowly. Her hair isn't falling out as much now with the new medication. We have a doctor's appointment next Friday to follow up. I'm praying for good news."

Cathy squeezed his arm. "Please keep me posted. Rosa's a strong woman. I'm sure she'll overcome this."

He nodded, giving her a warm smile. "Thank you."

"You don't have to come next week. I'll see you in two

weeks," Cathy said and noticed the worry lines on his forehead. "Don't worry. The payment won't change. I figure you could use that time to be with Rosa. Besides, I live here alone. How much of a mess can I possibly make in a week?" She knew most people hired a cleaning service every two weeks, but she kept Victor and Rosa on once a week. She liked them and didn't mind supporting their business. They had been cleaning for her mom before Cathy hired them for her own house.

His eyes watered. "I don't know what to say."

"Say that you'll make the best of it. Life is short, Victor. Be with your family when you can."

After Victor left, Cathy resumed her work. She tried to take the same advice she gave to others, which was why she planned a three-week vacation to regroup. She hadn't taken a break in a long time, so this vacation was a treat. Her best friend, Sydney, the vice president of Luminous Press, could manage while Cathy was away.

Cathy planned on using this extra time to brainstorm the greeting card collections for the next few seasons. Designing the art for the greeting cards was one of the fun parts of her business. It activated a different area in her brain that wasn't crammed with numbers, profit margins, production, deliveries, and so on.

A bird squawked somewhere, and the unique sound broke through the silence. She rose from the deck and glanced toward the woods that drew her to this place. Beyond the trees was the gorgeous Prudent Lake. She had brought a tent out there a few times and slept under the moon and stars. She was due for another adventure soon, especially with the August Moon Festival next week.

When she was six years old, she looked out her bedroom window at the full moon and saw a gold rim around it. It glowed for a while, mesmerizing her. At that time, she had felt a warmth brush against her face when the rim glowed, but it could've been the imagination of a child believing in magic and fairytales. Because of that childhood experience, Cathy felt an odd friendship with it. The moon pulled at her in an inexplicable way.

With nature as her background, Cathy found the stability to move on after her mother's death a year ago. They used to come to Prudent Lake on vacation when she was little, so living here was somehow reliving the precious moments they'd shared together. She had no idea where her father had gone. He left when she was six, and that broke her mother.

Another squawk rang out, and she looked around, trying to see the bird or hawk that was making the lovely sound. She spotted nothing. She went into her kitchen, took out the bag of birdseed, and filled her bird feeder. "Enjoy your snacks."

She loved watching the birds gathered in her backyard like it was their playground. The enchanting sounds of nature were the spa that relaxed her.

Her phone rang, and Sydney's name flashed on the screen. "Hey, I don't mean to interrupt your vacation, but I just wanted to remind you about the August Moon Festival next Friday in Boston. Are you going?"

The August Moon Festival was a special time of the year for her family and her heritage. In the past, she'd attend the event with her mother. But this year, Cathy wanted to do something personal, something without the crowd. She could celebrate the holiday right in her backyard.

"I'm going to pass. I'll just do something small at home."

"Are you sure?" Disappointment leaked from Sydney's voice. They had met in college and became fast friends.

Cathy appreciated Sydney's intelligence and foresight when it came to business. Outside of business, Sydney was the trusted friend every woman deserved. Without Sydney's support in both business and friendship, Cathy didn't know if Luminous Press would be as successful as it was.

"Yes, I'm not in the mood for crowds this year."

"Hang out with us girls," Sydney said. "We love talking shit about cheaters, and there's *a lot* of them. That means we'll have plenty of conversations and drinks."

Cathy laughed, appreciating her friend. "We'll hang out soon, I promise. I need to hire a contractor to finish my studio. I want to get it done before I return to work. And I'm brain-storming the new greeting card collection too."

"You're *supposed* to be on vacation," Sydney said with a disapproving tone.

"Yes, *Mom*. I know, I know. I don't mind it, though. The creative part is fun for me. You know that."

"I do, and that's why I'm not driving over there and dragging you away. Do you want me to bring you back any mooncakes, lanterns, food, or anything?"

"No, thanks. I already placed an order for the mooncakes. They're being shipped to me. Have fun, and don't forget to make your wish to the Moon Goddess. You never know. She could make your dreams come true."

"I'll be sure to make a long list for her. She should find something on there to give me," Sydney said.

"You are the queen of lists." Cathy could imagine the several pages of demands from Sydney.

"Hopefully, the Moon Goddess won't find me too high-maintenance. I only want intelligent, sexy, humorous, and thoughtful men to come to my door. I'll even settle for their snores and messiness." She let out an unladylike laugh. "Maybe we're doomed, Cathy. Maybe we're meant to be alone, which I don't mind now and then. But sometimes I miss that connection, you know? What happened to all the decent men who wanted gorgeous women with acute intelligence and creativity?"

"We're not doomed," Cathy reassured her best friend. "We're special, and special things are rare. 'Decent' men are rare too. We just have to wait for our turn. In the meantime, live life. Have fun. The right guy will come along. You're a fabulous catch, and you need someone who measures up to you. Don't ever lower your standards to be with someone."

Though Cathy offered words of encouragement to her friend, a part of her wondered if there was a decent man out there waiting for her. After her failed relationship, it was hard to believe in happily ever after.

"This is why Luminous Press is successful," Sydney said. "You always turn the bitter into beauty. We make fabulous journals and greeting cards that give people hope."

"Hope is the lantern that gives off light when you need it." Cathy didn't know why these deep thoughts were spewing out of her so easily.

"Oh, I just thought of something!" Sydney said with excitement. "What do you think of these for Valentine's Day cards? *Do you want to be my lantern? I burn for you. Let me light you up! Let's illuminate the night together.*" She giggled. "They're cute and cheesy, but I have a weakness for that stuff."

"I think they're perfect." Cathy grinned into the phone, admiring the creativity of her friend. "I'll let you handle the next Valentine's Day Collection."

"Cute and cheesy, here I come."

Their conversation carried on a few more minutes before Sydney had to run to a meeting.

Cathy tucked her phone into the back pocket of her shorts, picked up the hammer from the deck, and dropped it into the pouch of her tool belt strapped around her waist. She strode over to the unfinished addition on the side of her house, which also shared the same deck. With hands on her hips, she envisioned the complete studio that would allow her more space to create.

Another squawk erupted nearby. Cathy glanced over to the tree next to her just in time to see a splash of glistening white feathers disappear into the woods.

What kind of bird was that? She loved discovering strange animals and rushed down the steps in the hope of catching the bird. Hoping it perched somewhere close for her to peek, Cathy made her way into the woods.

About ten feet in, she didn't see anything and headed back to her deck. As she walked, a strange sensation pulled at her. She wobbled a bit and blamed her imbalance on the lunch she missed. She got caught up with all the hammering. She glanced at her phone; it was already six in the evening. It was time for dinner. *Shit.*

She got back onto the deck and was about to enter her home to make a sandwich when she heard the squawk again. This time, it sounded further away, but the call echoed through the woods like gentle music that penetrated through the clutter of your mind, catching your attention. Not only that, she heard a loud swoosh of wings flapping somewhere. A powerful gust of wind carried an interesting scent to her nose. Was it citrus or sage? She wasn't sure, but she liked the aroma. It soothed her.

She waited a beat to see if she could hear it again, but silence reigned. Was it her imagination? Or was there some large bird out there? Perhaps it was someone's exotic pet that had gotten lost.

She'd investigate after she fed herself.

TWO

Daedriel

One flap of wings and he soared across the serene skyline, over dense trees and sparkling lakes, taking in the mesmerizing view of Earth. He glided through the air, letting the wind massage his face and feathers.

In a horizontal position and ten feet above the water, Daedriel glanced at his reflection. Dark hair, a cream T-shirt, black leather pants, and iridescent blue wings glistened against the glassy surface of the lake. His blue feathers darkened from the warm colors of the setting sun. One set of wings flapped and allowed him to soak in the fresh air that invigorated his lungs. The other two sets of wings rested in their invisible state. There was no need to exert more energy than necessary. The air on Earth was denser than that of the Celestial Realm, but his body could transmute the air quality to suit his need.

As a seraph from the twelfth-dimensional matrix, Daedriel possessed power more potent than any other angels—even the Archangels, who were his friends. Well, some of them, anyway.

He smirked, knowing that if they heard him, they'd object and challenge him to a duel until all their feathers were destroyed in the battle. But those days of carefree play amongst friends hadn't been around for a long time. He missed it, but there were important priorities now. The battle to protect the Celestial Realm had intensified and thus tossed all the angels into defensive mode. The threat to their home and their existence hung in the balance as darkness multiplied within the Universe.

The Celestial Realm was a sacred place within the twelfth-dimensional matrix that was also a doorway to higher dimensions. Some he had visited, while others remained a mystery to him because to get there required an energy boost he didn't have. What he possessed allowed him to travel up to the fifteenth-dimensional matrix. His responsibility to rein in the darkness kept him busy enough from the twelfth dimension and below.

The darkness continued to infect and distort the Celestial Realm, which was why he was on Earth trying to locate the traitor, Rask. He had once been a trusted guard, but he stole the Reversal Black Tourmaline, a rare gem infused with darkness. A regular black tourmaline crystal absorbed and neutralized negative energy by turning it into nothingness, giving that energy a new beginning. But dark powers had manipulated one black tourmaline eons ago, reversing its natural abilities. The Reversal Black Tourmaline had absorbed and stored so much dark energy that it became a weapon for the dark side. The dark could pull power from that stone to feed itself.

Years ago, the seraphim angels had won it back from the dark. They brought it to the Auric Circle, where powerful celestial forces extracted the darkness to be alchemized slowly, naturally. To destroy such a powerful gem could wreak havoc on all life forms.

Where was Rask? Daedriel had tracked his energy to this place known as the state of New Hampshire in the United States of America. Of all places, why was Rask here on Earth, in a land filled with trees and lakes? Was Daedriel being misguided? That thought crossed his mind several times, but he trusted his instincts. Something here was calling him, and he had to find out what it was.

As he neared the home he'd just bought two weeks ago, his pet parrot, Tika, flew up to greet him.

"You're late." The white parrot squawked with its purple beak, gliding beside Daedriel. The pair of white wings glistened with a pink hue from the setting sun. "Did you know you have an interesting neighbor? She's human."

"We're on Earth, and humans live here. Aren't you supposed to be watching the energetic screen for any signs of disruption? We have to find Rask and retrieve the Reversal Black Tourmaline."

"I was. But then I heard loud noises in the woods, so I went to check. That's my job, isn't it? I'm supposed to investigate if something doesn't seem normal and notify you."

Daedriel sighed, knowing it could be a long conversation with Tika's ability to talk on and on.

"What did you find out?" Daedriel landed on the balcony of his house and folded back his wings. The modern home was built by an architect and contained all the amenities that were useful for Daedriel. He'd spent an obscene amount of money on the purchase. He needed to be at the center of this place where dark energy pulsed strongly. But there was another unidentified source of energy that called to him.

Daedriel shifted his wings into invisible mode and stared at his parrot. "I'm listening. What did you find out? And be quick about it."

"Well, it was nice seeing you too." The parrot gave him a

look similar to an "eye roll." Tika was a celestial creature that could mimic beings around him.

Exhausted from the hunt for Rask, Daedriel wasn't in the mood to chit-chat. He had flown along the eastern coast, trying to locate his enemy. The fact that Rask could've already used that stone infused with dark energy twisted Daedriel's stomach. He didn't want to think about that catastrophe.

But if Rask had used it, Daedriel would have felt the shock waves. The energetic disruption would have interfered with Earth's frequencies. The release of extreme malice and menace from the Reversal Black Tourmaline would open a gateway for more evil to enter and reproduce on Earth at an exponential rate. The dark energy held within this stone came from dangerous beings that wielded potent powers. Darkness existed everywhere. It knew how to maneuver and manipulate energies to suit its needs. The Reversal Black Tourmaline was the steroid needed to empower itself.

Daedriel couldn't let that happen here on Earth—a place already immersed with so much suffering. On a third-dimensional matrix, Earth was more vulnerable than other planets that existed on a higher frequency. Humans who were weak in their minds and hearts would be affected most. The teeth of evil would sink into them, turning them into willing soldiers to expand cruelties.

Damaat. Where the fuck was Rask?

"I'm tired, Tika. I've been searching for the bastard for two days."

The parrot made a sound and jumped onto Daedriel's shoulder. "We'll find him, Dae."

A noise echoed in the forest, and the vibration caressed Daedriel's skin as if calling him. That caught his attention immediately. Ever since he'd been on the earth plane, he hadn't experienced this odd phenomenon. The energy on Earth was heavy. He had to use more energy to cut through the density here.

He strode toward the edge of the balcony, staring toward the direction of the neighbor he hadn't met. As he honed into this strange force, he recognized a familiar moon aspect. This feminine energy had a connection to the moon.

In all of his immortal life, he hadn't met a being that radiated this kind of moon frequency. Was this the unidentified energy calling him?

"I sense the moon in her—whoever she is," Daedriel said more to himself.

"I know. That's also why I flew over to her house to see what she was doing."

"What was she doing?"

"Hammering at the wooden board on her back deck and mumbling to herself." The parrot flew over to the ledge of the balcony. "Humans are interesting. They're so *dramatic*. Thanks for taking me on this trip to Earth so I can see for myself."

"It's not a vacation, Tika."

"I know. But I'm learning from pure observation. Anyway, there's something different about her. Your senses are better than mine, angel warrior. So I figured I'd let you know so you can acquaint yourself."

"Acquaint myself?"

"You're here to search for Rask. This is Earth, so the playing field is different. Maybe if you make some human friends, they can help us. Then we can go home and resume our lives."

Tika didn't understand that darkness had changed everything, and searching for the traitor was one of many tasks his seraphim brothers and he were doing. But his parrot friend didn't need all the gloomy details. Daedriel wanted hope to continue perching on his friend's soul. Hope was the thing that kept everyone going. Despite how much Daedriel wanted to give Tika the truth, he understood that some truths were best kept hidden for now.

His mind whirled to his human neighbor. Tika was right; Daedriel could use some human assistance.

But how was he supposed to acquaint her?

THREE

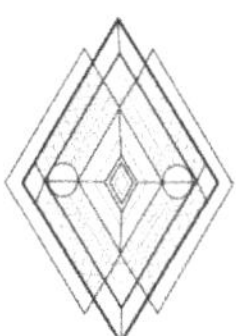

Cathy

She pounded another nail into the wooden beam of the railing that led to her incomplete studio and missed her mark, hitting her index finger.

"Oww! Shit!" She dropped the hammer to the floor. Her finger throbbed, and she blew on it as if that would help. It didn't.

Maybe that was karma for thinking ill thoughts about Gavin earlier. She thought the turkey sandwich she ate for lunch would have given her some equilibrium back, but apparently, clumsiness still lingered. She should call it a day.

Twigs crunched and caught her attention. She looked over toward the woods, and a stunning man stared back at her. He had chin-length dark hair that glinted like black metal against the warm colors of the setting sun. The tips of his hair glistened with a bluish hue. She didn't understand how that was possible because the dense trees prevented much of the sunlight from filtering through, especially during the evening hours. Regardless, an attractive man was standing on her property wearing a cream-colored T-shirt that showed off his muscular arms and black leather pants that made her mouth dry. She shivered from his stunning appearance. His athletic physique showed he took care of himself, which meant he had discipline. She appreciated anyone who put in the effort for what mattered to them.

"Are you okay?" he asked.

His voice carried a baritone that woke up nerves in her body in ways she hadn't felt before. Had she screamed that loud to have a stranger checking on her?

Cathy glanced at her throbbing finger, the pain diminishing slowly. "I'm fine, just a minor accident. I'm Cathy Lu. Do you live around here?"

She knew the three neighbors that lived on her street, but she'd never seen *him* before.

"You can call me Dae. I recently purchased that home over there from the architect. I was just taking a stroll to check out my neighborhood. I haven't had time to look around the area since I bought it."

"Oh, right. Jason and his family moved to Europe. It's nice to meet you, Dae."

Without invitation, he strode up the stairs, meeting her. "What are you doing?" He surveyed her deck, the hammer on the floor, and the tool belt around her waist. "You're handy."

With a hint of pride, she shrugged. "Not really. I'm just trying to get some things done before I narrow down the list of contractors to finish this big project." She pointed to the studio that only had an exterior structure and a partial roof. All the interior construction needed work. "I need someone to finish that for me."

Dae walked over, peering through the window. "You still have a lot to do. What are you using this space for?"

"My studio. I own a publishing company. This space will

allow me to work from home on days I don't feel like going in." She sighed, and for some reason, she thought about her mother. "Besides, it's for my mom. It's to commemorate her."

What was wrong with her? Why did she share this personal detail with a stranger who probably didn't even care? The nail had slammed into her finger, not her head. Where was her caution? She must have been working too hard today; all sense of logic seemed to have disappeared.

Dae nodded with understanding. "That's a nice gesture. I'm sure she'd be very happy." There was something about him that spoke to her. She didn't know what it was yet, but she was intrigued.

This man drew her in with his dark hair tipped with iridescent blue, a color she hadn't seen on anyone. Maybe he dyed it?

"Do you live here with your family?" Cathy asked.

He ambled closer, revealing blue eyes that were incomparable to anything on her color palette.

"No, just me and a pet. How about you?"

"I live here alone. I enjoy the solitude."

"Solitude is a good thing," he said, glancing toward the woods. "There are so many hiking trails here, I don't know where to start. Is there a map or something that can help me?"

Cathy remembered thinking the same when she first came to this place.

"I do have one. Have a seat, and I'll get it for you." Cathy gestured to the patio chair. "Would you like anything to drink? Coffee, tea, orange juice, or red wine?"

A smile stretched across his handsome face and flipped her stomach sideways. Her usual routine didn't include inviting strangers over for a drink, especially a man she just met minutes ago. But something urged her to be friendly. Besides, he was her neighbor, and she wasn't inviting him *into* her home. They were on her back deck. If something were to happen, she could scream loudly again. She kept her tool belt on just in case. She had screwdrivers in there that she could whip out in seconds to defend herself if needed.

She couldn't stop studying his handsome face. It begged to be admired. She was just complying with the language of beauty. Was there such a thing? At this moment, there was, and she was the one who made it up.

You're being ridiculous, Cathy. She knew it, but she couldn't help wanting a few minutes to stare at his beautiful features and sculpted body.

She wasn't making any sense. She wasn't acting on logic. She was *reacting* to something she didn't know. Maybe the hammer had slammed on a sensitive nerve in her finger linked to a part of her brain, disengaging the portion that monitored practicality and safety protocol.

"Coffee is great, thanks."

When the coffees were ready, she strode back out with two mugs and a map tucked in her tool belt. She didn't need any more caffeine if she wanted to sleep early tonight, but she figured she could use the time to think about the color scheme for the greeting cards. Owning a business means it lurks in your mind even when you're on vacation.

"Here you go." She placed the white mug and map in front of him.

"Thanks." The corners of his eyes crinkled. He took the map, glanced at it, then tucked it into the back of his pants, returning his attention to her.

The dynamic blue portals of his gaze drew her in. She couldn't look away. She didn't want to. She broke eye contact because it was rude, and it was... confusing her. How could he make her yearn this much when she hardly knew him? She wasn't like this with Gavin. They had met through friends, and she didn't remember experiencing this inexplicable attraction to him.

Why was it happening now? Was it because she hadn't been with anyone since Gavin? She wasn't desperate, and she had things that occupied her time.

Cathy pushed those thoughts aside and sat across from him. She removed her tool belt, placing it on the table. "I'm sorry, I didn't mean to stare, but you have the bluest eyes I've ever seen. It's like cobalt blue with some electric blue in it."

"It's a *celestial* blue," he said, sipping his coffee.

Cathy considered the name and smiled. "That works."

He placed the mug down. "The tool belt looks good on you."

Was that a compliment? She didn't feel attractive in her dirty shorts, sweat-drenched T-shirt, and black hair twisted into a messy bun on top of her head with a pencil stabbing through it.

She shrugged. "It's useful, practical. I'm sure yours is a lot bigger and can carry more tools."

Even his nod had an interesting flair to it. Maybe it was just her fascination that made her notice everything. He had a fine-boned face that demanded attention, a face that appeared to have been molded from tough times and pressure, a face that portrayed ancient wisdom. How in the hell did she even come up with that? It was his eyes that held wisdom and stories. An intelligent man with a unique story could teach her something. Curiosity was her weakness.

How could he be single? Just because he lived by himself didn't mean he wasn't with someone. Why was she thinking about that, anyway? She was supposed to be keeping her distance from men, especially a man with such an irresistible face. His mouth had a perfect masculine curve that made her wonder how effective it would be on her body.

She blinked at her bold thought. She grabbed her coffee and took a generous sip, not caring if the heat would burn her tongue. Maybe the heat would keep her mind out of the gutter.

"Can I see your hand?" he asked.

"What?" The odd question surprised her. "My hand?"

He jerked a chin adorned with a slight stubble to her injured finger. She'd forgotten about it. The reminder brought back the discomfort.

Cathy didn't know what to do.

"My hands are clean," he said. "I just want to see if it'll bruise. I've injured my fingers before, so I can take a look."

Cathy didn't see any reason why he couldn't examine her finger. "Are you a doctor or a nurse?" She placed her hand in his palm, and warmth bloomed at the skin-to-skin contact. Her reaction was not the result of the hot coffee. She watched with keen interest as his long fingers examined her injured one. His rough skin brushed against her smooth surface. The discomfort she felt disappeared, and he released her hand.

"No, I'm not a doctor. Your finger won't bruise. If you're still looking for a contractor to help you finish your studio, I'm handy, and I'm open to the project."

"*What?*" Her eyebrows furrowed. He lived in a beautiful home that cost millions. He didn't appear like someone who needed a job, especially one that required sweat and manual labor.

The questions probably displayed on her face because he said, "I'm not in need of a job, but I can make an exception to help out a neighbor. In exchange, I hope you can help me too."

Oh, he's a businessman. What does he want to negotiate?

She weighed the pros and cons of hiring him. It would be convenient for him to work. He lived next door, and she could monitor him and ask questions if they arose. She didn't mind looking at him while she worked in her small office upstairs either. It would be a lovely view. But a small part of her warned that hiring him could lead to problems she wasn't ready to deal with yet. Even though she wasn't ready for another relationship, she was open to having fun. Hadn't she just given the same advice to Sydney? She had to practice what she preached, right?

Cathy had a life to live and keeping all her doors shut was not living.

And right now, Dae was the reminder she needed that there was joy and beauty around her. If she didn't take this opportunity, it could disappear and never reappear again.

"Do you have a portfolio of your work?" Cathy asked.

He leaned into the table, and the celestial blues flickered. "You're a cautious businesswoman."

"Caution is required when dealing with an unknown businessman." She smirked, looking into the woods. The more she stared into his eyes, the more she wanted to know him. This was already moving too fast for her comfort. "I don't normally invite strangers onto my deck for coffee on the first day. I broke that rule today."

"Then I should consider myself lucky. You were being neighborly."

She flicked him a glance. "And illogical. You can't trust everyone. People wear masks." The comment was meant more for herself than him. She didn't even know why she said it.

His expression changed, and though questions swam in his eyes, he didn't ask them. She was thankful because she had no intention of discussing the past with him.

Dae rose from his seat, appearing larger than he did before. Or was her perception all skewed?

He stood about six foot three, taller than Gavin. His wide shoulders made her think of a strong, horizontal beam that supported the weight of a fine structure. There was a slight blue hint to his sun-kissed skin that accentuated his biceps even more. It couldn't be the spotlight from her house, could it? Maybe his powerful blue eyes radiated color onto his skin. That was a bizarre idea, but it was the only explanation that made sense to her.

"I'll send some images of my work for reference. I've retired from architectural work, but I take on small projects when they interest me. So feel free to ask questions. Let's exchange contact info. Okay?"

Curiosity piqued at his mention of retirement. He didn't appear that much older than her. What exactly did he do for now to occupy his time? Or was he one of those people who had several jobs, and retiring from one didn't mean anything?

"Sure." She gave him her cell phone to input his data, and she did the same with his. His phone seemed heavier than hers even though it didn't look any bigger. She dismissed it to the fact that her hand was injured.

"I'll send them over tonight," he said.

"Take your time. Just so you know, I'm very picky, so if I don't take your offer, please don't be offended."

"Of course. I like a person who knows what she wants. I wouldn't want you to regret anything."

Cathy pursed her lips. "The studio construction is a huge project to take on. What kind of help would you need from me?"

Those lips curved again, and her body shifted into alert mode. "How about we worry about that after you see my work? There's no point in discussing the terms if there's no project involved, right?"

She nodded and gestured to the map in his pants pocket. "I can give you a tour of the trails tomorrow. That's a neighborly thing to do. Is noon a good time for you? I have some stuff I need to prepare for the August Moon next week, or I'd offer to show you around in the morning. It's too dark right now." She glanced toward the woods.

Dae angled his head. "What are you doing for the August Moon celebration?"

He knows about this holiday?

That fascinated her more than anything. The August Moon Festival wasn't a holiday that everyone knew about. It was a celebration for many Asian countries. Cathy's ancestors came from China and Vietnam, and the celebration of the moon during this time was similar to Thanksgiving. It was a time for the family to celebrate the harvest and to share magical stories. Depending on the culture, the legends varied a bit about the Moon Goddess and the animals that lived on the moon. As a child, Cathy was enamored with these fantastical stories that made her wonder and gave her hope.

"You know about the August Moon? That even though it's an 'August Moon,' it's celebrated in September on the Gregorian calendar?"

He rocked back on his heels and smiled. "I do know. The August Moon is also referred to as the Mid-Autumn Festival that's celebrated in August on the lunar calendar, which follows the moon's monthly cycles. That's usually a month behind the Gregorian. I also know that various Asian cultures celebrate the holiday differently. It's interesting to see how people come together on this full moon night. Celebration is a beautiful event. It generates joy, and joy pushes out 'unjoyful' things."

She was already intrigued by him before, but now she was elated that he knew about her culture. He just moved to the top of her must-get-to-know list of interesting people. His knowledge of this holiday meant a lot to her. It was one of her favorite times of the year. He just proved that he was more than a handsome face, but rather, a cultured man.

Dae didn't appear like a regular good-looking guy. He stood

like some angelic warrior that emanated magnetism like no one she'd met before. Something about him called to her; something subtle yet so powerful, she couldn't ignore it.

"I'm preparing for the celebration. If you're interested, I can show you what I'm doing tomorrow."

"I'd be honored."

After Dae left, an odd emptiness filled her deck. He had a presence, and when he left, that warmth left too. Her body craved something it didn't even know. Did that make sense? No. She shook her head at how strange the day had turned and decided a cold shower would clear her mind.

But as she showered, she couldn't stop thinking about her neighbor. Who was he? Why was he retired at such a young age? Was he loaded with money? Was he a trust fund kid? Or was he a criminal hiding away in this small town of Prudent Lake?

A smirk grew on her lips, knowing the internet could give her all the answers she wanted.

FOUR

Daedriel

Heart pounding, Daedriel stalked into his home and shut the door. He placed a palm over his chest; his heart pulsed like a raging storm. The potent vibration was something he'd never experienced before. Over the years, he'd learned to keep his emotions locked tight in a safe place, where no one and nothing could jeopardize them. As a seraph warrior, he'd been in too many battles and had lost brothers and sisters. Though his angelic legion was immortal, they could be killed by another immortal or by those who had the right weapon.

His parents had been killed by a demonic immortal a long time ago. Their deaths had propelled him on a mission to eradicate all the evilness.

He'd seen too much darkness in his days, and the best way to protect his heart and his soul was to lock them in a place that couldn't be touched.

So why was his heart racing now? He glanced down at his trembling hands. The last time he trembled was when he discovered Rask had deceived his legion. But Daedriel wasn't angry right now. He was... he wasn't sure what he was feeling. Was it confusion, amusement, or a spark of joy that overwhelmed him? They all meshed together into one big discombobulation. He only knew that being close to Cathy had elicited this bewilderment in him. She had a face blessed with timeless beauty and brown eyes that looked like smoky quartz.

He strode into the living room covered with light-gray walls and dark wooden floors, where a single brown couch sat at the center of the room with a small coffee table. No other furniture accompanied them. He dropped down to the couch and inhaled a deep breath, releasing it slowly.

Tika flew over and perched on the arm of the couch, cocking his head. "Are you okay, Dae?"

His heartrate had slowed down a bit, which confirmed that it had to do with Cathy, a beautiful human who stirred him in unimaginable ways. She yanked at the latch on his emotion.

"You're right. There's something different about our neighbor," Daedriel said.

Cathy was an attractive female, but he'd seen many stunning females on his travels and had several lovers in the one thousand and one hundred years he'd been alive. Despite that, he had never encountered a female who affected his body and heart this way.

"I told you so." The parrot squawked, flying over to the tree growing from a pot.

Daedriel never imagined being attracted to a human before. His previous relationships involved other female angels or beings who knew that he preferred something temporary because he was always on the move. But now, a small part of him wondered if a forever mate was possible for someone like him?

Unlike the angels born from a divine stone, Daedriel had

been birthed from an avian being from the thirteenth-dimensional matrix. His grandfather had been a seraph created from the divine stone, but he fell in love with another seraph and gave birth to a baby seraph. Daedriel's father gave his heart to Daedriel's mother, an avian star-being. So Daedriel was a hybrid seraph, not that it mattered to his legion. They knew his heart and his purpose.

Another thought intruded his mind. What would it feel like to spend one night with Cathy? If she could move him this much without even touching him, what could she do to him with a kiss? If his intuition served him right, she had the power to destroy him.

If that was the case, then he should stay away.

But why didn't he want to? Why did warriors never back away from challenges that intrigued them? Because they wanted to know their limits. He wanted to know *exactly* what she could do to him. He had to know how to overcome this weakness so that he could move forward. Yes, that explanation made sense, he told himself.

A vision of her kissing him flashed across his mind like a shooting star. Though it was quick, it was enough to warm his blood, making him want that fantasy to be real.

Damaat. He cursed himself for the digression. He was on Earth for one mission only: to find Rask and the gem. He didn't have time for short-term relationships or fantasies. Relationships would split his mind in several ways, which would delay his search for Rask. Where was the Reversal Black Tourmaline?

Daedriel tried to focus on Rask's energy and the stone's frequency, but he couldn't tap into anything. Did Rask keep the stone? Or did he hand it over to someone else? What if someone else threw a mask around it, preventing Daedriel from picking up its energy?

"Something going on with you?" Tika landed on the wooden coffee table. "You seem off."

Daedriel looked at his pet, who read him well on certain days. "I think I just need a day to rest. Searching for Rask took a lot of energy from me."

He didn't want to discuss this strange new attraction to Cathy just yet. The conversation would be too long, and Daedriel wasn't in the mood for chatter.

The Celestial Realm and his legion needed him to focus on what mattered most. He had to push all urges aside to concentrate on the task at hand.

Furthermore, if he began any kind of relationship with Cathy, it wouldn't last, anyway. He was immortal, and she was mortal. That added a complexity he didn't need. From his experience with other lovers, he understood they always wanted more from him. They wanted things he could never give them.

He didn't have commitment issues. He just knew where his life was heading, and it involved a lot of darkness. As a seraph who would do anything for his legion, he was committed to his responsibility. But personal relationships were a different kind of battlefield he wasn't accustomed to.

Tika flapped his wings. "So, what kind of 'moon' thing did you discover from our neighbor?"

Daedriel fed his pet some information. "I don't think she knows that the moon's frequency surrounds her. She has an affection for the moon. It's like a belief that's been in her all along. That loving energy radiates from her."

"And you're a seraph who monitors moon frequency. *Interesting.*" Tika brushed a wing against Daedriel's arm.

"She's preparing for the August Moon celebration, and she invited me over tomorrow."

"That was fast." Tika made a sound similar to a teasing

squawk. "You must have been quite charming. Or she's too trusting."

Daedriel crossed his arms. "Charm is something I learned from you." He patted Tika on the head, giving him exactly what he needed. "She was being neighborly."

Tika puffed out his chest and walked back and forth on the arm of the chair. "I hope she can help us locate Rask or the stone. Maybe he's living in this town. Maybe she's met him. Maybe she could get us access into secured places."

Daedriel didn't think Cathy could help him with Rask. From his conversation with her, she didn't know about other-worldly things that existed around her. He didn't sense any negative vibration from her either, so Rask wouldn't be on her radar. Rask and those associated with the Dark Angel Agenda were attracted to individuals who shared negative energy. All Daedriel sensed from her was hope and love.

Despite that, Daedriel was fascinated by her, so he needed a reason to be closer. Why was her energy affecting him this way?

Daedriel didn't need Cathy to help him enter a place. He could go anywhere if he wanted to, but that required his use of seraph powers. To activate such a potent force would draw unwanted attention, letting Rask know that the seraphim angels were close by. That alone would be enough to make Rask run. It wasn't just Rask who Daedriel didn't want to alert; it was also the fallen angels from the Dark Angels Agenda who wanted to destroy the Celestial Realm.

The DAA was comprised of many dark beings from various worlds. Any negative beings that believed in the "agenda" of spreading darkness and extinguishing the light were welcomed into that alliance.

Daedriel had killed fallen angels, demons, negative aliens, and other creatures that belonged in the Underworld—a complex place with many problems. Even the Lord of Hell would have a tough time controlling these pockets of darkness that didn't want to be controlled.

The Dark Angel Agenda was one of many dark legions that the seraphim angels battled. The war between light and dark was a constant within the Universe. He vowed to protect his realm because, without it, life would be unfathomable.

Daedriel switched his thoughts to something that lightened his mood. "I negotiated a deal with Cathy. If I help her complete her studio, she'll help me in return." He didn't know how she could help him, but intuition told him she'd be of assistance one way or another. Sometimes, even a seraph had to rely on intuition for guidance.

Tika eyed him with golden eyes. "Did you tell her what kind of help you'd need?"

"Not yet. I just met her. I didn't want to frighten her with stories about demons." He rose from the couch and poured himself a glass of Lavandula wine and swirled it around, aerating the drink. This bottle of wine was from the private collection stored in his sanctuary. The light blue flesh of the Lavandula grapes sparkled, possessing a translucent appearance that was both beautiful and hypnotizing. This tasty fruit only existed in the Celestial Realm and in his private garden.

"And she agreed?"

Daedriel shrugged and sipped his wine, gliding the liquid over his tongue as he swallowed, savoring the balanced after-taste of sweet, sour, salty, and bitter elements. Cathy's lovely face interrupted his wine, making him want to share a glass with her.

"She wanted her studio finished, and I offered. She wants to see my portfolio first though. She's cautious. And she should be." He recalled how his heart pounded from her nearness. "I resonate with her energy. I think she can be helpful even if it's not directly linked to Rask."

"She's smart to be careful. I wouldn't hire you on the spot."

"I'll send her some images of my work later. It won't take me long to build her studio. I've built temples, castles, villas, monuments, all kinds of architecture before I stopped and decided hunting the dark suited me better."

"Not better. *Needed*. We needed the best warriors to fight the DAA."

Daedriel appreciated Tika's understanding. "Though I haven't built anything in a while, I haven't forgotten those skills. I'll show her a few examples and see if she wants to hire me."

The parrot cocked its head. "What exactly are you going to show her?"

"My best work, what else?"

"And you think she won't question you about the marvelous castles and intricate monuments that don't look like anything from her world?"

She would question him, but wasn't that his intention? He wanted more conversation with her. If they were going to collaborate, they had to know each other. Furthermore, he wanted to present himself in the best way possible

Damaat. Why should he care? He'd never cared about what any female thought of him. It never mattered before.

Daedriel didn't answer Tika, and the bird stopped inquiring.

"Will you introduce me?" Tika landed on Daedriel's shoulder, the claws pinching into his skin.

"Sure, but let's see if she agrees to the job first," Daedriel said. "If she doesn't, then you don't need to meet her."

"What if I want to?"

"Why?"

The parrot expanded his wings and hovered in the air. White feathers glistening with gold accents beat in front of

Daedriel's face. "Because she's the first female to intrigue you this much. I want to know who she is."

With that, Tika flew into the library, where he had his large tree branch secured between two bookcases and a cabinet full of food.

Daedriel digested Tika's words. Tika had been his friend for over three hundred years. Tika was one of the few beings who knew Daedriel well. He didn't object to Tika's perspective. Damaat, he agreed a hundred percent.

Daedriel finished his wine and snapped his fingers. The wine glass disappeared from his hand and into a dishwasher, joining the other dozens of wine glasses.

Needing time alone, Daedriel entered his office that seemed to only house one desk and one chair. After closing the door, he ambled over to the rectangular desk made from the Taram tree, which came from the Reeshi Rae Forest. He had brought the desk out from his private cache of favorite furniture, books, and artifacts.

With a wave of his hand, Daedriel pulled back the veil in the room, revealing two comfy off-white couches and a coffee table made from a slab of celestite crystal. Two large armchairs faced his desk, and unique artwork graced his walls, reminding him of places he'd been. He'd been here and there, traveling across the Universe into several planes of existences and time-lines. But none of them were his *home*. He had many temporary homes. None of which truly belonged to Daedriel of the Seraphim Angel Order. Like his brothers, he wandered around, making a home wherever the responsibility took him.

However, he had a sanctuary he often entered when he felt out of place. That was his home, his meditative ground.

Did he want a permanent place for himself? Why was he thinking about it? It hadn't even been on his radar until now. Until Cathy Lu, a woman he hardly knew. But she was someone who kept intruding his mind. It was as if he knew her from an energetic perspective.

Daedriel pushed all those thoughts away as he pulled up a virtual computer screen from the surface of his desk and reviewed the moons from across the Universe. This moon task used to be his responsibility until he joined the Seraphim Angel Order, which was created by Source. The alliance consisted of angel warriors who vowed to take down the Dark Angel Agenda. The DAA had killed someone important to them.

Daedriel had monitored the moons' frequencies from the twelfth-dimensional matrixes and below. Each moon conducted a different wavelength of energy that contributed to the balance within the Universe. When energies were in harmony, life flowed beautifully for everyone. But harmony was a goal difficult to achieve when the rise in darkness pushed the scale out of balance.

From monitoring the moons' vibrations, he knew when a moon was consumed with darkness, it sent out a blast of negative energy to the planet it orbited, affecting the behavior of all life forms, including weather patterns. The moon affected water, blood, and emotions. He'd seen many moons die in several dimensions over the years along with the civilization of its planet.

Even in his Celestial Realm, he felt the shift in frequency. The increased dark energy had deceived, lured, and corrupted celestial beings that had once promised to preserve that which was sacred. But power, greed, and other sinful intentions changed all of that. He sensed darkness nibbling at the edges of his realm, trying to create chaos whenever it could. If an inner soul wasn't strong enough to steer clear of distraction, it would fall victim to the negativity. Perhaps that was the case with Rask.

He'd seen how the darkness had manipulated the purity of

the moons throughout the realms. He glanced at the various moons on the screen, their different sizes, textures, and colors. Their beauty astounded him, and the way in which their frequency and gravitational pull impacted water and the overall energy levels fascinated him. When pure water was infected with dark energy, the fluidity took on a different behavior that could destroy the moon and those living in and on it. Having monitors assisted in preventing that catastrophe. Creation was a complicated and beautiful thing. He wanted to preserve that sacred beauty.

While Daedriel checked the overall scan of the moons' energies, he didn't notice anything abnormal. He shouldn't even have been checking it because he had delegated this task to his Archangel legion, who had offered to assist.

Next week was a full moon. What would that mean for him? When his mission aligned with the phase of the full moon, something came to fruition. Something completed itself. A part of him wanted to know, but another part feared it. As an angel, he shouldn't fear anything. But he knew what was out there, knew what existed beyond the veil.

Unlike the new moon—when the dark side faced the Earth—the full moon radiated the light from the sun, giving Daedriel an advantage. But this meant the black forces gathered their negative energy on the side of the moon that didn't have the sun's light. Darkness possessed an intelligence that knew how to use the phases of the moon to transmit their agenda. They could achieve this in various ways. One of them was by influencing the subconscious mind. Chaos often erupted around the full and new moon cycles.

Daedriel zoomed in on an image of the Earth's waxing moon and contemplated its significance to his life. Maybe he'd catch Rask and retrieve the Reversal Black Tourmaline. That would complete his mission.

Of all places to run to, why would Rask run to Earth? This couldn't be random. There was something here that Daedriel was missing. Why couldn't he see it?

He leaned back in his chair, thinking about Cathy, and joy sprouted in his chest. Giving his mind a rest from Rask, Daedriel scoured old architectural images of things he'd built over time. He gathered various examples from several timelines to showcase his structural ability. These images were taken from snapshots inside his memory palace. He sent copies of the chosen images to his enhanced mobile phone, with its reception and radar capabilities upgraded beyond human understanding. Humans had the product, and he had the power to manipulate it, allowing it to penetrate through several magnetic fields.

At midnight, he texted her images of his work and got ready for bed.

What would she think of him? Would she hire him to be her contractor?

FIVE

Cathy

Cathy slid into bed when her phone buzzed with a new message. She grabbed the phone from the nightstand. A message from Dae lit up, and her heart raced like a teenager infatuated with her crush.

Here are some images for your reference. Don't hesitate to ask any questions. Have a peaceful night.

She scrolled through the pictures, and her mouth dropped in awe. He sent her stunning architecture made of stone, wood, glass, and metal. She ogled over the modern and ancient designs that reminded her of the Petra in Jordan, the Mayan temples, and even the Hanging Temple built into the overhang of a mountain in China. She drooled at the exquisite details of three monuments that looked similar to the Great Pyramids of Egypt. She'd always wanted to visit these ancient sites. She blinked, making sure she was truly seeing these brilliant buildings.

Aside from those breathtaking structures, she also admired the modern homes that appeared high-tech with solar panels or some kind of electricity conductor on the exterior. Dae was a marvelous architect. He even sent her a few tree houses to review. But these weren't the same ones kids played in. These were innovative tree houses that people lived in—people with money.

Where was all of this impressive buildings located?

Cathy considered herself a resourceful person. It was how she became a successful business owner. But after her NASA-level research on Dae, she came up with nothing. She'd spent more time than she liked to admit on him. The name on his house deed—which she got from the city's public record—stated it was owned by SAO LLC. She couldn't find anything with that alias.

What exactly was his business?

She could ask him tomorrow. For now, she continued admiring his work. If he worked on her studio, there was no doubt the result would be exceptional. How much would he charge her? He mentioned that he wanted her help in exchange, but help with what? They had to discuss that detail tomorrow too.

Tucked in bed, she got the urge to reply to his text. Should she? Wasn't it strange to text your neighbor only a few hours after you met him? Especially at midnight?

But he had been the one who initiated it by sending her the first message...

Why was she complicating this matter? It was just a simple text message.

Thank you for sending the images. They're ABSOLUTELY stunning! Some of these buildings look ancient. When did you build them? And where in the world are they?

She waited a beat, not expecting him to reply. It was past midnight, after all. Maybe he fell asleep right after he sent her the images. She placed the phone down on her nightstand, switching off the light. Her phone buzzed as soon as her head hit the pillow.

She bolted right up and grabbed the phone, staring at the screen.

Thanks! Like any form of art, architecture tells a story. They're in small cities here and there. If you'd like, I can show you one of these days.

She'd love to. But that didn't answer her question. Maybe he had clients who preferred to keep their homes and corporations private. If she owned one of these buildings, she wouldn't want the public gathering around it either. So, she dropped the subject and asked another question.

Why are you retired? Your work is fabulous.

Cathy was now wide awake, texting with a man whose face and body were their own exquisite architecture.

I have other responsibilities that are more important right now. Does that mean I'm hired?

Cathy grinned at the smiley face icon he added.

Yes, you're hired. But what will it cost me?

Your help.

That's it? Her lips pursed.

That's it.

Help with what? She desperately wanted to know.

We'll discuss it tomorrow.

Okay, all details in person tomorrow. She had to make one thing clear. *I have some criteria, though. One, I'm not going to hurt anyone. Two, I'm not for sale.*

For sale? I don't understand.

Was he being coy? Did he want her to say it out loud? Well, it was better to text the message than to say it to his face.

I'm not going to sleep with you for money or for the project to be completed, if that's what you're thinking.

Dae took longer to reply than she anticipated. Maybe her statement threw him off. Or maybe she hit the nail on the head.

That thought didn't cross my mind, but it's an interesting idea. You'll be helping me with an investigation.

What was he talking about?

Like a detective?

Exactly. It's late now. You should go to bed.

You too. Come by around ten for some August Moon tradition.

What kind of investigation did he have in mind? Was the SAO LLC the name of a private investigation company?

SIX

Cathy

The next day, Cathy took out some patterned paper from her company stock and folded it into paper boats. With each boat, she placed a blessing for everyone around her: her friends, her coworkers, her business, her neighbors, and even strangers she didn't know. Why not? People needed help all the time, and if those around you were in harmony, that meant you were in that field too.

On one paper boat with floral designs, Cathy made a wish for herself. Perhaps the boat would take her wish to the Moon Goddess, or perhaps the boat would dock on some magical place that offered her clarity or something she never expected. What-ever it was, Cathy gave her trust to the Universe.

This was the tradition that she and her mom used to do every year to celebrate the Mid-Autumn Festival. Family tradi-tions were important to her mom, and Cathy continued that tradition because it kept her mom close.

With three paper boats and two lanterns in her basket, she headed down the stairs of her deck and out into her yard.

She felt his presence before she saw him. A surge of warmth entered her space. She glanced up, and the magnificence of him overwhelmed her. Dae wore a light blue T-shirt and light-washed denim jeans, and a pair of sneakers today. His eyes seemed even brighter than yesterday, and iridescent blue sparkled at the edges of his wavy black hair.

She stepped back and almost tripped over a rock. He reached forward and clasped a hand over her arm, stabilizing her. Heat radiated on her skin and slithered all over her body.

"You okay there?" A hint of a musky aftershave snuck up her nose, making her want to lean in for a better sniff.

"Yeah. Just a bit clumsy today. I had a late-night texting with someone."

"I did too." He smirked, releasing her arm, and her body yearned for it back. He glanced into her basket. "I assume those are your August Moon supplies?"

"Yup. Follow me." She strode into the woods, using a dirt trail. "Did you know that in ancient times, people made paper boats and sent their wishes out into the water? They did this with paper lanterns too." She stopped by a small stream that connected to Prudent Lake.

"That's a beautiful concept," he said.

Though she only met him yesterday, there was an odd trust between them already. Maybe it was just her, but she didn't fear him at all. There was none of the awkwardness that often came with a new friendship.

The silence in the woods embraced them and it was as if nothing else existed at that moment. The smell of moist dirt and fragrant flowers stirred around her. The sound of gentle water sliding over pebbles became music to her ears. The atmosphere soothed her, and it was precisely what she needed to start her day.

She crouched and gestured for him to do the same. "Every year, I fold and place my hopes and dreams into three paper boats and then release them into this little stream." She rose and walked down to where a pile of rocks sat. "I don't let them go into the lake. Even though these boats are made of paper, and they'll eventually disintegrate, I don't want to litter. Intention gives everything power, right?"

"You're very thoughtful," he said, watching the paper boats travel down the stream. "What are those?" He gestured to the remaining items in her basket.

"These are lanterns. Here, this is for you." She took one out from the basket and handed it to him.

"For me?" Shock splashed across his face as he stared at it like it was an alien.

"Why not? Let's head back to the deck. We need to assemble these. I'll come back for the boats later. They'll just hang out in this little rock lagoon I made for them down there."

On the deck, Cathy held up her paper lantern made of white paper. "This is a fun craft that kids love to do for the August Moon. Lanterns can come in animal shapes too. Some people write riddles on them. The young girls pray to the moon and ask the Moon Goddess to help fulfill their romantic wishes, hoping for happiness after a long year of hard work."

"The Moon Goddess must be very busy fulfilling all the wishes." He watched as she assembled her round paper globe and hung it on a string over her deck. He assembled a yellow paper lantern and hung it next to hers. "Did you ever ask the goddess to fulfill your wish?"

Cathy made one a long time ago. She had thought Gavin was the love for her. This year, she asked the goddess to give her what she *needed*. Maybe the goddess could see things Cathy wasn't privy to. In the meantime, she'd focus on herself and her career.

"I think it's a lot of work for one goddess to do. There are billions of people asking one deity. I'd be tired no matter how much magic I have." Cathy took out two LED candles and placed one in her lantern and the other in his. "No goddess would be able to fulfill all those prayers. No doubt, she'd miss a few."

"You didn't answer my question." He stepped closer, and his eyes sharpened on her. He stood so close that she could see the gold specs swirling within his blues irises.

Desire darkened his pupils, hypnotizing her. She didn't even realize she'd reached up to brush away a lock of dark hair covering his eyes until his hand clasped over hers, bringing it to his lips for a gentle kiss.

Energy zapped her skin, sending a thrill that rippled down her spine one vertebra at a time. Her body jerked in response, craving more.

"Did you?"

"What?" Cathy didn't know what he was referring to. Her mind only held the vision of those fine lips on her skin.

"Did you ask the goddess to fulfill your wish?" he repeated.

Oh, that question.

"She missed my prayer. It's okay. I can wait. She knows what's best for me."

"And what is that?" His voice lowered to a distinctively sexy tone.

A kiss from you would be best right now.

At that moment, Cathy decided she didn't want to wait for any deity to give her what she craved. She would take this kiss to satisfy her curiosity. One kiss would be enough. One kiss wouldn't be the end of the world.

She rose on her tiptoes and pressed her lips to his. The soft connection was like a meet and greet of day and night, acknowledging each other's presence and significance. His soft lips nibbled hers as if savoring her flavor. The delicate kiss soon became urgent, as if she ignited a hunger in him. The same hunger he sparked in her.

He pulled her closer, and with one hand on her back and the other cupping her neck, he kissed her senseless. His mouth took and took. She moaned, opening her lips wider for him. His tongue slid in, claiming hers like a warrior in battle. She tasted a hint of coffee, citrus, and something ancient. It didn't make any sense, but that was the thought that came into her mind as she slipped into some magical world where sensations spiraled in her. Heat exploded in her body, and she shuddered.

An eerie squawk sounded nearby, and he broke the kiss, whipping his attention to the large blackbird perched on the ledge of her deck. It was the size of a crow, but it had two heads.

"Oh, shit." Cathy bumped into the table. Was she dreaming? A creepy two-headed bird wasn't typical.

The bird squawked and beat its wings, flying away. But Dae grabbed a screwdriver sticking out from her tool belt—which still lay on the table—and whipped it at the bird. The bird wailed and dropped to the ground. Dae hopped over the deck railing and rushed over to the fallen bird with such speed that he couldn't be a private investigator.

Cathy approached him. "What was that thing?"

"An evil bird."

Another squawk sounded, but she recognized this pleasant sound. She looked up to see a white parrot the size of a hawk landing on Dae's shoulder. "Everything okay?"

Cathy knew parrots could talk, but the way this bird spoke with such clarity surprised her. "You can talk."

"Hi, Cathy. I'm Tika."

"Hi..." She stared at the stunning white parrot with a purple beak.

"Tika's my pet," Dae said, swerving his attention back to the dead bird.

Fearful nerves churned in her stomach. "What's going on here? What kind of bird is that? Why was it here?"

"Don't worry about it. I'll explain everything later. Right now, I need to take care of the dead blorvus."

How could she not worry? There was a two-headed dead bird lying in her yard with a screwdriver sticking out of its body. Meanwhile, a majestic-looking parrot that could speak with clarity was studying her with cautious eyes.

"You should go inside and stay home for the day," Dae said.

Her brows furrowed from the commanding tone. She wasn't used to people telling her what to do, especially a man who didn't give her much detail.

"Why? I have a lot of unanswered questions."

He released a slow breath and looked at her. Energy pulsed from his body over to hers. Was it normal for her to feel this powerful force of whatever it was between them?

The kiss. She needed a quiet place to think about that later. Right now, her mind was on the unbelievable event she had just witnessed. "I'm not dreaming, am I?"

"No, you're not." His eyes warmed on her but steeled when he glanced back at the dead bird. A pool of black blood stained the dirt.

A lethal blaze replaced the warmth that had been in his eyes, hardening his features as if he shifted into someone completely different from the man who had assembled the paper lantern with her.

"There's danger lurking around here, and I want you to be safe. Go inside and stay there. I need to get rid of this blorvus." He met her gaze, eyes warming again. "I'll be back to explain everything."

SEVEN

Daedriel

After Cathy went into her house, he turned his attention back to the blorvus. He tapped into his power, drawing out his sword of blue flames with a metal handle made from an alien alloy called fortisium. He stabbed the demonic bird's head, allowing the blue flames to devour its body. Then he withdrew the sword, waving it around the area. The blade of blue flames expanded, and long whips of energy snaked around, eating up the darkness where blood had pooled. The flames cleansed the soil by removing all demonic residues that came with the blorvus.

The blorvuses were birds from the Dark Angel Agenda. They created various demonic creatures to carry out their mission to destroy good across the Universe and all its dimensions. Daedriel had killed blorvuses before. If he hadn't killed this one, it would've flown back to where it came from and reported his presence.

Daedriel had cloaked himself with a layer of protective energy that suppressed his seraphim energy. But that kiss with

Cathy shifted him on a colossal level that he could still feel in his blood. That huge spark created a tear in his magical cloak, allowing his seraph energy to seep through. The power she ignited in him was so strong, his six wings almost expanded from his body without his command. He had to patch up that cloak later.

During the kiss, he couldn't stop himself from wanting her. For a moment, he forgot who he was. He forgot he was a seraph on a mission. All he had wanted was *more* of her. One kiss had changed everything for him. That one kiss had altered the life of a seraph.

Damaat! If he could undo it, would he?

No. The quick answer shocked him. In all the years of his long life, Daedriel had never felt this alive. That one kiss made him crave more of the joy he'd once loved. The joy he'd tucked somewhere deep inside him. But he didn't have time to think about that.

Daedriel forced his mind back to the matter at hand. Had the blorvus sensed the seraph energy that leaked from his cloak? How many more were out there? He should've been more careful. Darkness lurked everywhere. He couldn't risk the DAA sensing his angelic force nearby. They would alert their allies and attack him. Nothing was more attractive to the Dark Angel Agenda than an opportunity to destroy an angel.

He stared at his seraph fire devouring every part of the blorvus. Like all his brothers from the Seraphim Angel Order, Daedriel possessed seraph fire that reflected the color of his wings. These flames were a gift from Source to assist in the fight against the Dark Angel Agenda. It could destroy the darkness, turning it into nothingness—a clean kill, leaving no residue behind. But the use of that power drained Daedriel's well. Rest and wine would replenish it soon.

Tika squawked and perched on a nearby branch. He had

returned from monitoring Cathy. "She's safe inside her kitchen. But she's looking out this way. She's curious."

"Thanks for the update," Daedriel said. "It's about time she knows who her neighbors are."

"The blorvus sensed you. *I* sensed you. More might be coming. What happened earlier?" His parrot landed on the ground. "There was a big energy shift."

Daedriel didn't want to share his intimate moment with Cathy. He had inadvertently put her in danger because he couldn't resist her. He couldn't resist the mouth that tempted him or the fact that his body moved toward her before his mind could say no.

How was he going to explain to Tika that a seraph warrior was vulnerable around a human female? She wasn't just any human female. She was Cathy, and she had immense power over him.

If the DAA sent another agent here, they'd know what Cathy meant to him. He couldn't hide what pulsed from his heart. Want and need pulsed in his blood. His heart had never pounded harder than when he was with her. During the kiss, energy ricocheted from his heart and coursed through his body, alerting his bones to prepare for the six-wing expansion.

"That was me," Daedriel admitted. "I should've been more careful."

Tika flapped to another tree, surveying the area. "She's the reason you came here. You sensed it all along."

Daedriel nodded and deactivated his sword, the blue flames blinking out in an instant. "I need to transmute the energy to make sure it's as clean as possible."

He connected to the energy swirling in the pit of his stomach. It traveled up to his body, spiraling toward his skull and heating the optic nerves behind his eyes. Two beams of blue seraph fire shot out from his eyes, burning the soil. He let the flames enter Earth's crust and go where they needed to clean out dark energy. Embers floated around and disappeared.

He closed his eyes, cutting off the beams of fire. Then he opened his eyes and whirled around, focusing on the surrounding energy. He didn't sense any darkness and was finally able to relax.

Daedriel strode back into his house and glanced at his watch. It was only noon, and so much had happened, so much had changed. He poured himself a glass of Lavandula wine and admired the sparkles that emerged from it. He swirled the blue liquid around and sat on the stool beside his kitchen counter. He needed something to calm his mind.

While he savored the flavor, he tossed a few scenarios around in his head. How should he explain what happened to Cathy? What should he share? He didn't want to overload her. A gentle introduction to his world was best. But where should he start? Would she be terrified to know the truth about him?

Nerves prickled at him, and he didn't know why. Fighting demons didn't make him nervous, but trying to explain his purpose on Earth to Cathy did. She mattered to him. What if she didn't want anything to do with him because of his association with the dark? What if she told him to go away?

How should he disclose the information about the blorvus? And what about Tika?

Tika wandered across the marble kitchen counter and stopped in front of him, lifting a wing. "What are you going to tell her?"

His bird read him well. "I need to relay the information gently so she can understand it. Too much might frighten her, shock her. I don't want that."

Tika cocked his head. "Did you see her face? She's already shocked. She just wants answers."

Daedriel hadn't expected to explain to anyone why he was

on Earth. He came to Earth with one mission: apprehend Rask, retrieve the stone, and bring them both back to the Celestial Realm. It should have been a simple journey. But things had gotten more complicated.

"She's going to understand better than you think. I see it on her face, in her eyes. There's an inner strength that radiates from her. You would've noticed if your sexual energy weren't *tangling* with your brain."

Daedriel slid a warning gaze at Tika, but said nothing. Though his parrot wasn't wrong, Daedriel didn't appreciate the snide remark. As far as he was concerned, his sexual energy was his business. Wherever and however it tangled was his private matter. What did a parrot know about an attraction between a seraph and a human anyway?

Regardless, he had sensed pain and suffering from her, especially when she spoke about her mother. Grief was a claw that dug so deep, it left marks. He understood that well. The death of his parents was the reason he dedicated his life to fighting the dark.

He also sensed something else: disappointment or betrayal, he wasn't sure. Emotions were universal frequencies, and he had over a thousand years to hone that skill set. Even so, emotions were tricky when they were personal.

But inner strength didn't always predict how someone would react to full disclosure of beings and creatures from another dimension. He was used to beings from various dimensions, but she wasn't. Humans lived in a world where the density of energy created restrictions for them.

Maybe Daedriel was overcomplicating matters. He only wanted to protect her, ease her into his world.

What was he supposed to do now? These feelings for her were too strong for him to ignore. Even as he sat in his home, he could still taste her on his lips. He'd never forget the flavor that was her. His heart pounded again, and he knew the truth was the only way to move forward.

"I'll tell her one truth at a time and see how she takes it." He slid off the stool. "Do you know where I left my tool duffle bag?"

"Why?" Tika squawked.

"Besides killing creatures from the DAA, I also have a studio to build, remember?"

EIGHT

Cathy

As she paced her living room, Cathy wondered when Dae would come back and give her some answers—anything—that would explain the bizarre event that just occurred before her eyes. A chill raked down her body from the memory of the two-headed blackbird. It was like some kind of mutant creature.

She even searched online for any information about two-headed birds, but nothing useful came up. Of course there weren't any two-headed birds on Earth. She just needed something to make sense of it all.

Her mind wandered back to the kiss she shared with Dae— the best kiss she'd ever experienced. Her body still trembled long after he was gone. She took in a huge breath and released it slowly. She didn't know if her agitation was from the bird or the kiss. Both had unraveled her in different ways.

The freaky bird was like a creature from a nightmare, and the kiss was a storm she didn't see coming, but it was exactly what she needed to clear her mind. It allowed her to see that she still had the capacity to *want*. Because during that kiss, all she wanted was more of Dae.

How could she desire so much from someone she didn't know? That frightened her. Was she losing her self-control?

Despite those insecurities, desire grew like a flame that couldn't be doused.

What would his hands feel like skimming over her body? Heat skated down her spine as if his fingers were touching her at that moment. This sudden need baffled her, but it confirmed that she had moved on from her previous relationship. Dae ignited something deep within her that she didn't even know existed. Now that the flame had flickered, she couldn't ignore its illumination.

The sound of footsteps on her deck caught her attention, and she rushed over to peek through the window.

Her heart raced from seeing Dae. He dropped a huge duffle bag on her deck.

She rushed out, delighted to see him. "Hi. What's this?" She pointed to the bag.

The worried expression from earlier had disappeared from his face. He jerked his chin to her studio. "Tools for the construction."

With the frightening event, she didn't think he'd remembered. "You still want to help me today? I assumed you'd want to focus on something else."

"I keep my word. I told you I'd help you, so I will." He came up closer to her, and a zing of energy zipped through her.

What was wrong with her? Why was her body *so* sensitive around him? She'd never felt her skin or muscles react this way.

She glanced down at the massive duffle bag that was three times the size of her tool belt. "What do you have in here? It's huge."

He crouched, unzipped the bag, and pulled out a silver

hammer that gleamed from top to bottom. In a blink, the hammer glowed and multiplied into three hammers, all different sizes that wouldn't fit inside that duffle bag.

Cathy gasped as the three hammers flipped in the air and became one again. "Did I just see three hammers? Or was it some kind of holographic trick?"

"It's angel magic, more specifically, seraph power." Dae reached for her arm, and warmth stamped her skin. He led her back to the patio table and chair. "Have a seat, and I'll tell you a story."

Cathy sat, but his words still hung in her brain. "Did you say seraph? Like a type of angel?" She thought she had questions about a two-headed bird, but now she was more fascinated with an angel story.

She waited for him to smile and laugh everything off, but he didn't. She waited for him to admit that he was a special effects tech from a nearby movie set, trying to tease her. She would have been okay with that.

But the admission never came.

She considered herself an open-minded person, but this was something that required a lot more brain space to comprehend. Could it be possible that the things she used to read about in books were real? She'd always been fascinated with mystical things, which was why she loved stories that were passed down from tradition, why she prayed to the Moon Goddess even though she didn't have any proof that the goddess was real. Believing in something beyond herself gave her hope and wonder.

Cathy folded her arms around herself, afraid of the unknown, but wanting to know the truth. She didn't think there was anyone else more confused than her right now.

He shifted his chair to face her and sat down. The blue eyes illuminated into a gorgeous hue she'd never seen before. "My name is Daedriel. I'm a seraph in search of a traitor who's hiding on Earth."

Cathy opened her mouth, but she didn't know what to say. A traitor? Monsters and demons automatically popped into her mind. Fear bubbled in her stomach, but as she stared into the magical portals of his eyes, the fear vanished.

She had so many questions, but started with one she'd been curious about.

"What's the difference between a seraph and an angel? I'm not familiar with heavenly stories, and I have a feeling that what I've read in books aren't accurate depictions."

The smile that curved on his lips was sexy and devilish. She'd probably reserved a spot in hell for associating such things with angels.

"You're right about that. Books are wonderful to learn from. But the truth to anything is something you need to *feel* within you." He placed a hand over his heart. "Stories are told by someone, and that someone is subjective in their interpretation. It's just how things are. We mold stories that align with our personal beliefs. That belief is not always the truth. The storyteller can be anyone; a human, an angel, a vampire, any shifter, an alien—"

"Wait a minute, *an alien*?" She didn't know why that threw her off, but it did. On the list of fantastical things he named, that stood out to her because she'd never imagined them to be real at all. Not that she imagined any of the others were real, but she'd seen them in several movies before, so she was "familiar" with them.

He shrugged his shoulders. "Why not? There are various 'beings' out there that you don't know about. You live in a different matrix than us, a different dimension. I've encountered and collaborated with other life forms to help maintain the peace across the Universe."

The subject matter and the serious expression on his face

told her that her life would no longer be the same. She just stepped over that invisible line that separated the new Cathy from the old version who had never met an angel. She waved farewell to all the things she had learned before this moment, making room for the truth that she wasn't sure she was ready to accept.

Yet, she held the door open for whatever came. Because right now, she was sitting with a seraph who wanted to tell her an unbelievable story.

"I believe you," she said, inhaling a deep breath. "People put their own spin on things, and before you know it, the truth is buried underneath layers of opinions and disagreements."

She thought about the current state of America and the world. There were so many conspiracy theories, and people fought over things that made no sense to her.

"Are you sure you're ready to hear what I have to say?" he asked. "If not, I can hold off."

If she wanted to understand things, then she needed the truth, even if the truth hurt. Her last relationship flashed in her mind. If she had discovered the truth sooner, it would have saved her from heartache, embarrassment, and shame.

"I'm ready."

"Unlike other angels, seraphim angels have six wings."

Cathy recalled seeing something like that in one of the art museums she'd visited. "Why six? Do they make you fly faster?"

He let out a laugh. "We're stronger, and we do have better speed than those with two wings. In your history books, they'll say that the seraph uses his top wings to cover his eyes and his bottom wings to cover his feet. The middle set is used to fly. Why? A 'normal' seraph is the closest angel flying around God or Source or whoever you believe Him or Her to be. Because a seraph is so close to the 'mighty' light, he needs to cover his eyes, so it doesn't blind him. It's like being close to a blazing sun.

There's too much power there." Daedriel pointed to his sneakers. "Feet are used to walk on the ground, where they pick up dirt and debris. So the seraph doesn't want that debris to be around what is considered 'perfect.' Does that make sense?"

Wow. That blew her mind wide open. She wanted to ask if he'd seen God—if that light was male or female—but she knew the answer. She remembered him saying that the truth was something you need to "feel" within you. He was right. Belief made everything real, so it didn't matter if that higher power was male or female. What mattered was how it translated to the believer's heart and what that person did with that belief. She'd witnessed how people manipulated things to benefit them.

"Wow," she said out loud. "I had no idea it was that complicated."

"There's more to it, but I'm keeping things broad, so it's easier to comprehend," he said. "Your books have some truths correct. The role of the six wings isn't just to cover my eyes and feet. They're useful in battle, especially when I'm traveling through several dimensions. If one set of wings were damaged, I could use the other pair in combat. I don't always expand all six."

She gaped at him. "How many dimensions are there?"

"As far as I know, there are forty-four. I can only travel up to the fifteenth. But I've heard new dimensions are revealed when Source is ready to disclose it."

"There are hierarchies within the Universe?" She supposed that was required to keep things in order.

"I like your inquisitiveness." His eyes glimmered. "The beings who reside on the higher dimensions have more power and are responsible for various things in the Universe. Source is connected to all dimensions, which means you can access this mighty power if you open yourself to it. Think of it as a life force. It exists in you. It is part of you."

"So I can talk directly to God, Goddess, or whoever I believe is my Higher Power?"

He nodded. "Yes. You don't need to go through anyone else. It's that simple, and that's the truth." He tapped his heart. "Angels have emotions like humans. Anything with consciousness can feel. But because we exist on a different frequency, we can discard negative interference easily, whereas humans have too much density to cut through. We're prone to many of the same things as you are, like desire, love, and betrayal. We're just more aware of our consciousness, but that doesn't stop some of us from falling prey to the dark side."

Cathy tried to imagine the complexity of the Universe. She probably only knew about one percent of what was out there. "How do angels or divine beings keep everything in check?"

"There's a benevolent 'police force' that's always around, enforcing the laws of the cosmos. This has been going on for a long time. The seraphim angels are a faction within this benevolent 'police force.'"

Cathy couldn't help the next question. "So where does the darkness come from? Hell?"

"Now, this is a complicated topic. Different cultures have different views of what Hell is. The Underworld is where darkness thrives. But you have to understand the various aspects of darkness. There are several kinds, and not all of them are evil. A beautiful, calm night is dark, but it's quiet and soothing in its own way. I know the current ruler of the Underworld, and he keeps the demons in check as best he can. But evil is a disease that can be born outside of Hell." Dae gestured to his head and heart. "It's born in individuals who are not strong enough to fight off the dark whispers. It grows from within, and that is how the dark feeds itself. It feeds on weakness."

Cathy's eyes widened. "You *know* the Devil?"

"Ralston is an interesting character, and he's not like the one you read about in your books."

Hope surged in her as her mom's face popped into her vision. "If there's a Hell, then there's a Heaven, right? Can you see people who have passed? Do they all live in a peaceful place up there?"

His eyes warmed. "Heaven isn't what you think it is. Yes, it's beautiful there, but it's what we call an Interdimensional Hub, where good souls travel through to reach their destination. No one knows what that destination is. It's a private discussion that often happens with the Lord of Karma. This 'hub' is for all beings, not just humans. In the spirit world, everything and everyone is energy. There are no physical faces for you to see. If you happen to see a spirit visiting you, it's because they chose a form you're familiar with."

Tears glistened in her eyes as she comprehended his explanation. "So the souls are getting ready to be reborn?"

"If that is their choice. They can choose to remain as energy up there, watching over you. They have a choice."

That knowledge gave her peace. "Can you visit it?"

He shook his head. "No. I protect the Celestial Realm, which is a massive twelfth-dimensional field. The Interdimensional Hub is one section of it."

"Oh." She appreciated his explanation more than he could ever know. "Thanks for explaining that to me." She met his gaze. "I have a feeling my mom is probably hanging out with my grandmother right now cooking up all kinds of meals. I'm sure those passing through the Interdimensional Hub are gaining a few pounds from their cooking."

Laughing, he said, "I'm sure they are."

After taking a moment to absorb everything, Cathy swung her attention back to Daedriel, a name she loved saying. "What do you mean by 'normal' seraph? Are you one?"

Daedriel shook his head. "I'm not a 'normal' seraph who stays in the Celestial Realm. I'm a hybrid seraph. My father was a seraph, and my mother was an avian star-being. She's an alien from an avian star race that has wings. When I was born, I had two wings. My parents placed me on a divine stone that activated my seraph DNA to awaken the other two sets of wings. When my parents died in battle, I joined the SAO, Seraphim Angel Order."

Her heart ached for him. She knew what it felt like to lose a parent. "I'm sorry to hear about your parents."

"Thank you."

Cathy remembered the name from her research of him. "You used SAO for your business name in the public record to purchase your house."

A perfect dark eyebrow lifted—and why did she find that attractive?

"You investigated me?"

"I had to make sure my neighbor wasn't a serial killer or some criminal. What exactly does a seraph from the SAO do?"

A smirk slanted on his lips. "We battle the dark forces, eliminating them before they get close to the Celestial Realm. We travel across the Universe into different dimensions to ensure the darkness stays at bay. Like I mentioned earlier, we're a faction of the benevolent police force. We target the most extreme darkness."

Her stomach churned uncomfortably, trying to imagine all the evil creatures she'd seen in movies. "So you're constantly in danger."

His eyes softened on hers. "Are you worried about me?"

She bit her lip, not knowing what to say. She didn't want to admit to anything yet. She was still trying to understand her emotions. "I worry about all my friends."

"Do you kiss your friends the way you kissed me?" He

leaned in closer, and she stopped breathing for a second.

"I don't kiss my friends!" she retorted with vehemence.

A cocky grin that shouldn't have looked sexy on an angel formed on his lips. "I thought so. Then we are *more* than friends." The firm statement hung in the air between them like an invisible lantern no one could see, but could feel the flame burning from within.

His arrogance shouldn't have been attractive, but she melted from his confident expression. Perhaps confidence in a seraph was more compelling than in a human.

"I chose to be part of the Seraphim Angel Order. The more forces fighting the dark, the better. If we don't keep the dark in check, darkness will expand everywhere, including here on Earth. I know Earth isn't perfect, and darkness has already infected a large portion of it. But it could get worse."

Cathy understood that statement well. The history books got one thing right; the battle between light and dark had raged since the beginning of time. That brought up another question.

"How old are you?"

His eyes flickered. "One thousand, one hundred years old. I'm considered a young seraph."

Her mouth dropped open in disbelief. She studied his stunning face, the tan skin blessed by the sunlight, the thick dark hair that made her fingers itch to touch, and the muscular body that exemplified power.

"You don't look your age."

"I'm immortal."

The sadness that welled in her stomach shocked her more than the fact that he could live forever.

Without her.

They'd shared one kiss. Nothing had really started between them. So why was she overwhelmed by this sadness?

Maybe it was the squashed hope that made her sad. She had

hoped that this "thing" between them could be something more. But now, what was the point if the duration of their lives were so different? Soon, she would age and die, and he would live on.

She didn't want to think about it anymore, so she changed the topic. "What was that two-headed bird? Why was it here?"

"That's a blorvus, an evil bird that works for the Dark Angel Agenda. The SAO is trying to eliminate them."

"Are they like fallen angels or something?" She wasn't completely clueless.

"Some are, and some are hybrid beings. They're very powerful and intelligent. They know how to manipulate positive energy, turning it into negative energy."

"I guess the books were right about your angelic realm always battling demons. If I were to look in a book for your name, would I find Daedriel?"

He smiled. "No, you won't. Seraphim from the SAO aren't mentioned anywhere because we're a covert order. I like it that way. The Archangels are better known. They're like the 'social media' representatives for our angelic realm. Everyone prays to them, asking for things. Michael often gets headaches from the onslaught of prayers. It could get overwhelming. He delegates some of the prayers to the other angels in the legion."

Cathy laughed, imagining an Archangel with a headache. How many painkillers would it take to obliterate an angel's headache?

"You guys hang out often?" she teased.

"Back in the day, we did. But now, we're all busy running around fighting the darkness."

She glanced around. "Are they... here? The fallen angels, the evil creatures."

His jaw tightened. "Darkness is here in your city. The dark can shapeshift, take over weak souls. It often hides among the wealthy and powerful because the 'glamour' is its mask. Darkness has been here for a long time, but the light is here too, fighting them." He swallowed, and his eyes steeled. "I tracked a traitor named Rask to Prudent Lake. That's why I bought that house. I didn't know how long it would take me to look for him."

Revelation dawned. "Is that why you need my help? To look for him? What does he look like?"

"That was part of the reason why I asked for your help. You live here, so you might've encountered someone who seemed off. Rask can shapeshift and take over a human body as a host. But it weakens him if the host has a good soul. The personality of the host would change completely because the mind and soul are frozen while he's in control."

"Wouldn't he be able to tell if a soul is good or bad? It's obvious he's going to choose someone with energy that resonates with him, right?"

He leaned back in his chair. "Someone going through difficulties might lose their faith. Someone without faith lowers their barriers to everything, therefore, letting their guards down. When the doors are wide open, a negative spirit can start manipulating the mind, completely shutting down an individual's awareness. When that happens, a greater evil can enter and take over the body. But what the evil spirit doesn't know is that the soul has an energetic signature to it. This signature is your core belief. It resides in the deepest part of your heart, your soul. It's a form of energy that can't be changed even if it's dormant. It is what it is because you've harnessed that goodness over the years. So once an evil spirit takes over that body, the soul will find out."

Cathy thought she had heard every baffling thing today, but apparently not. "But people experience hardship all the time. I've dealt with grief and betrayal. Does that mean I'm more susceptible to evil?"

"No, the evil spirits need a certain amount of darkness or

'heaviness' for a duration of time before they can attempt to take over. Your awareness of who you are—even when you're grieving—protects you to an extent. Most people are aware of sorrow and disappointments and know that those emotions will eventually pass. Even when a dark spirit enters the body, you regain control again once you become aware that something is different. The more powerful dark forces require different methods of removal."

She tried to think back if she'd noticed anyone in her circle who had seemed unusual. "I'll keep that in mind when I'm out running errands." She looked at him. "What was the other reason for my help?"

That cocky grin again. "So I can be closer to you."

Joy burst in her stomach. "I didn't realize angels could be cunning and *devious*. It's almost sinful."

Lines crinkled in the corners of his eyes. "I'm not a regular angel. I'm a seraph who enjoys bending the rules, and I often break them when necessary. I don't play by the rules because the dark beings I'm after don't follow the rules. Rules are just guidelines, and as an angel in the field, I'm constantly formulating new ones." His voice lowered. "Despite that, there is one rule I don't play with."

"What's that?"

"Free will. It's sacred across all dimensions. The Celestial Realm values it. The fallen ones love manipulating it."

"So you were 'formulating' a new rule when you agreed to finish my studio construction? You gave me the 'free will' to hire you?"

Perfect white teeth gleamed with his smile. "I can't resist a smart woman who can read my mind." He leaned in and kissed her, dragging an open mouth across her cheek to her ear, and whispered. "You have a way of making me 'formulate' new rules to suit my needs."

Need slammed into her core. "Are there rules preventing an angel from being with a human?"

He nibbled on her ear, and tingles dripped down her neck like orgasmic honey.

"Not that I know of."

Her mind couldn't think. She was too focused on what he was doing to her neck and her shoulder. A low moan escaped her.

He pulled back, looking at her. "There's something powerful between us—something I can't and *won't* ignore. I want you, but I won't rush you. I'm leaving that fact out there for you to think about. If you think this isn't going the way you want it to, let me know."

He got up from the chair, strode over to his duffle bag, retrieved an intricate tool belt, and wrapped it around himself. He strode into the studio and took out a gleaming state-of-the-art nail gun. He lifted a wooden beam from the pile on the floor and began nailing it to the wall as if nothing had happened. As if there was no kiss. As if they hadn't just discussed the most complex topics from angels and demons to heaven and hell.

Cathy sat for a moment to calm her racing heart. He revealed he wanted her. He gave her the free will to choose what she wanted. Maybe it was an angel code that respected her ability to decide what was best for her and not him.

That in itself earned him more points than anything else. In only a few words, he made her feel more worthy than she'd ever felt. Her heart cracked a little, like an open window, letting in more light and fresh air.

For the first time in her life, Cathy felt like she was on the right path and that nothing could hold her back.

Inspired, she headed to her office to work on her greeting card collection, leaving her stunning seraph to construct her studio.

NINE

Cathy

Cathy worked in her upstairs office for the next three days and made progress on her greeting card collection. She chose the type of paper and the color scheme. She even wrote some words for the interior portions.

She'd taken a few breaks and wandered over to her window, glancing down at him more times than she should. Sometimes she saw him, and other times she only heard banging. Daedriel had added several interior walls, painted them, and installed more windows to her studio.

Daedriel left her alone to work, and she didn't bother him either. Neither of them mentioned anything about the sexual tension between them.

Though Cathy kept busy, Daedriel stayed in her mind. How could she not think about him? He was a seraph building her a studio. She was still trying to wrap her mind around it all. She replayed their conversation so many times in her head, and yet, it still baffled her.

What did he look like when his wings expanded? She envisioned six wings and wanted to see them in real life. Would he show them to her? What did it feel like to fly?

She should have been focused on getting some work done, but he was a fantastic distraction. She was supposed to be on vacation, wasn't she? She deserved an escape for her pleasure. No one had to know her thoughts.

Did he have a female angel lover? The thought gave her a stomachache, so she stopped.

She grabbed a pencil and began making a rough sketch of wings.

The blorvus intruded on her thoughts, and the stomachache worsened. Why was that horrid bird in her yard? Did it pick up on Daedriel's energy, or was it already here for something else? She'd lived here for two years, and she hadn't seen anything out of the ordinary.

A chill skated down her body, and she tried to force herself to concentrate on work. She couldn't ignore the fact that something was brewing in her neighborhood. Or was this anxiety stemming from their kiss and conversation?

Those questions were too big for her to answer, so instead, she wondered how her finished studio would look. She wanted the room to have a warm and open atmosphere, where ideas could flow uninterrupted like energy in a room. Her mom was great with Feng shui, which created beneficial energy flow in a space to attract joy, wealth, and good health. Her mom had taught her the basics. Cathy wished she had paid more attention, but she did remember a few useful tips.

She needed a bigger desk than the one she was using. She already had a new office chair in her storage. Some plants to produce more oxygen in the studio would energize the place. She took out her phone and began a shopping list for her studio.

Daedriel's kiss invaded her brain, and she stopped making

her list. *Fine.* Why was she ignoring this desire? Who was she kidding? Ignoring something didn't mean it wasn't there. She was attracted to her neighbor, who happened to be a seraph. She wanted another kiss from him, a longer one.

Cathy had never imagined she'd encounter an angel. Now that she had, reality shifted under her feet, tossing her into a magical place that was both here and there. He was "there." In a world she didn't understand. She was "here" on Earth, a tangible place that she knew well. But did she know it well? Or was she simply being shown one aspect of it?

It was hard not to wonder about that stuff. After meeting Daedriel, her mind traveled beyond Earth. That one kiss pushed her curiosity even further than before. Stretching the limits of her imagination would help her greeting card and journal business for sure. Aside from that, it was the quiet tugging in her heart that worried her.

One kiss with an angel changed her. The yearning she felt for him unsettled her. The power of it pushed all her emotions aside. Despite that, Cathy had learned from her mistakes with men. Daedriel was more than a man, which meant he had the ability to hurt her even more.

What kind of adventure was she in for?

It had been a while since she'd experienced anything this mind-blowing. But an angel who lived next door and was currently working in her studio was a phenomenon. It was true what the people said about the impossible being possible. She was experiencing it firsthand.

When a bird chirped a lovely sound, she walked over to the window. An adorable sparrow perched on a branch where an empty bird feeder dangled. Another bird friend arrived, also looking for food.

"Sorry, guys. I'll need to pick up some birdseed for you."

The birds chirped as if replying to her and flew off. Unlike before, when she had no interest in bird flight, today she focused on the wingspan of these sparrows.

What does it feel like to fly with wings? To have control of how fast or slow you can go? To be free and unrestricted? To be able to go anywhere?

She found herself wondering too many things about Daedriel. Did he feel free as an angel? He had responsibilities with the Seraphim Angel Order. Responsibilities could make a person feel trapped. She understood that too. She loved her business, but at times, those responsibilities restricted her. Did Daedriel possess those vulnerabilities like humans?

He was an angel, and that meant he had more power. Could he simply use some angel magic and make all his problems disappear? Could it be that simple? Fairytales would say so, but Cathy had a feeling that fairytales bent the truth to make kids feel safe.

She shifted her position at the window, trying to get a glimpse of him. She couldn't see him, but she heard more banging. She was about to walk away when he stepped into view, shirtless and sweaty.

Her heart leaped and her loins tightened. Sweat glistened on his sun-kissed skin, making his body appear almost metallic. She loved how his muscles bunched and lengthened with so much power. When his biceps flexed, her insides did too. This man, this angel, could elicit feelings from her as if he owned them. He was gravity, and she was a woman who couldn't resist his pull. A man with that kind of power was a danger to her heart.

How many hearts had Daedriel broken? Her chest tightened. Daedriel disappeared from her view again.

Confusion crowded in her tummy like weeds squeezing

through the cement cracks. Cathy had never been an uncertain person; she knew what she wanted and went after it. And if what she wanted turned out to be rotten, she'd toss it in the trash.

That was what she had done with Gavin. Lesson learned, moving on. But with Daedriel, her emotions were everywhere. It was hard to know which way to go. Should she move forward, or should she back away?

Logic told her to step back, to review the whole situation as if she was looking at a business plan. Would this relationship yield a positive result? Her body's reaction to him was a different matter. It wanted her to jump him. She smiled at the image of her jumping him, climbing that masculine body sculpted over a millennium.

Her mortality flowed across her mind. Cathy thought about her mother, who was no longer here. She shouldn't think about things that took the beauty and joy from the moment, but she couldn't help it. Cathy wished she had spent more time with her mom instead of clinging to regrets.

If Cathy's mom stood beside her right now, her advice would be to do what made her happy. *Stop complicating life.* Those had been her words.

Happiness could be fleeting, and she had to grab it when it presented itself.

If happiness were wings, she wanted to fly. If Daedriel was the flight, she wanted to soar with him.

An idea sparked in Cathy's brain, one that had her laughing. This new concept was her way of "simplifying" life. She glanced up at the sky, hoping her mom could hear her. *See? I'm still listening to you.*

Cathy had never done this before, but the novelty of it excited her. Would Daedriel find her intentions devious and improper? Did she care? If she was going to have fun, this was the time to do it. The Mid-Autumn Festival was a time for celebration, and Cathy was merely celebrating her desires. A wide smile spread on her face as she imagined various ways to seduce her angel.

She grabbed her purse, took a cold bottle of water, and headed to the new studio.

TEN

Cathy

Still shirtless, Daedriel stood outside the studio with his back to her, surveying the roof and gutter. Up close, his skin glistened a delicious bronze that covered the lean muscles. Depending on the angle, a hint of blue glinted from his skin. His dark hair fell over his face, lending him an air of mystery. Heat and power emanated from him.

"Hey. How's it going? Would you like a cold drink?" She offered him the bottle.

He turned, smiled, and took the bottle from her. "Thanks."

He gulped down the entire bottle and tossed it into her recycling bin on the deck. "Your studio is practically done. It just needs some light fixtures. I can do those tomorrow and clean up. Your roof is finished too."

Cathy walked around to where she could see her entire roof, turned, and gaped at him.

"How did you get everything done so fast? It's unbelievable." She looked at the exterior stone façade that made her studio look better than her home.

"I love building things, and I'm good at it. I could've used some seraph power to speed things up even more, but I didn't want to."

"Why not? Wouldn't that have saved you time?"

"It would. But magic pulls from a well inside me that needs replenishing. I would rather save that power for something else. Sweat and hard labor make you 'feel' the work; make you appreciate the structure you're building. You put in the effort when you care about something. Am I right?"

Her heart leaped. Was he saying what she thought he was?

"Are you saying you put in all this hard work to show me... you care?"

He held her gaze. "Why not?"

Cathy didn't know how to respond.

Daedriel strode to the door, opening it for her. "Come in and take a look."

Cathy's heart sighed with satisfaction and joy as she stood in the middle of the conference room. The studio consisted of three rooms: the conference room, her office, and the bathroom. She hadn't ventured inside because she wanted to let him work in peace. She hadn't expected him to make such quick progress. He exceeded her expectations.

All the walls were painted, the windows, lights, and wooden floors installed. The built-in bookcases that lined two walls in her conference room looked more beautiful than she'd imagined. She had given him a rough sketch of what she wanted, but Daedriel's exceptional skill had transformed them into masterpieces.

She ran her hand over the dark wood, empty shelves, and cabinet doors. Her mom would've *loved* these bookcases. Cathy hadn't been sure if she wanted to spend the extra money for them, but now, looking at the gorgeous bookcases that would showcase her journals and greeting cards, she knew she had made the right decision.

This finished studio represented a new beginning for Cathy. It commemorated her mom, who'd believed in Cathy and helped make her dreams a reality. The man who built this for her was an angel. Gratitude overwhelmed Cathy, and she tried her best to hold back her tears, but they came anyway.

She choked out the words. "Everything looks fabulous. Thank you." She wiped the tears away quickly, not wanting Daedriel to see her like this.

Daedriel came up to her and offered a paper towel he tore from the roll on the shelf.

"Thanks."

"You're welcome," he said. "I'm glad you like it so far."

"I *love* it. You did a spectacular job. I'm speechless."

Daedriel lifted a large wooden desk and placed it against the wall near the entrance. The way he used his entire body to move and lift things pushed her desire for him to the forefront. She wanted to feel those muscles on her body.

"I made something for you," he said, taking her hand and leading her into her office, which was the largest room in the studio.

"Oh my gosh," she gasped, placing a hand over her thumping heart. Surprise and elation rose inside her. A beautiful desk in the shape of a crescent moon sat near a wide window. She rushed over and examined the intricate woodwork along the outer edge that wrapped all around the elegantly shaped legs.

"This took the longest to build," he said.

She admired the striation on the gray wood. "It's beautiful... so magical. It looks like it's from another world." She ran a hand over the surface of the desk, and the striations shifted, forming other abstract shapes.

"It is," he said, standing beside her.

She whipped a glance at him. "What do you mean?"

"It's made from the Taram, one of the sacred trees inside the Reeshi Rae Forest. The tree produces plasma fruits."

Cathy imagined him cutting down part of a sacred tree to build something for her, and her stomach twisted uncomfortably. "Will you get in trouble for taking part of it to make furniture?"

He laughed. "No. The tree regenerates itself."

When did he travel back to his realm to get his supplies? But then she remembered he was an angel who could fly, probably entering some magical portal that took him to wherever he wanted.

She couldn't believe she had a piece of celestial furniture in her office. "I've never seen pristine craftsmanship like this." She walked her fingers along the smooth edge as though they were having a private conversation with the desk. No man had ever gifted her something so precious, so *meaningful* before.

It touched her soul. "You created this desk... just for me?"

"Who else would it be for?"

"It's a very special gift—something extra that wasn't part of the deal."

"Not everything needs to be part of a plan, Cathy. I prefer going rogue." Leaning against the desk, he tucked his hands into his front pockets. He stretched out his long legs, crossing them at the ankles. "I figured you needed a desk. It was the only thing missing on the blueprint."

Heat and power emanated from him as he stood next to her. Her body sparked to life. Her skin tingled as if she'd been zapped by an electrical charge. She stepped away a few inches so she wouldn't combust.

"I didn't know what kind of desk I wanted, so I left it out. But this design is better than I ever imagined. Thank you."

"You'll need to get a chair. Unless you want me to make you one."

She appreciated his offer, but he'd done enough. "I already have a chair sitting in my storage."

His eyes landed on her purse. "Where are you going?"

The entire reason she'd come down to see him flooded back into her mind. "I'm heading to the grocery store to buy stuff to make us dinner. I want to thank you for... all of this incredible work. We can discuss how I can help you in return over a home-cooked meal. Would that work for you?"

He beamed. "I'd love that." He pushed off from the desk and walked toward the door. "There's one more thing you need to think about."

Unsure of what he was referring to, she followed him out.

"You could add a nameplate or something here." He placed a hand over a section on the exterior wall.

Cathy hadn't thought about a nameplate, but it was a cute idea. "You think about everything, don't you?"

He shrugged. "Details matter. Take your time. We can add that after everything's done."

Cathy pursed her lips. She wanted something that carried his celestial energy because he had built it for her. "How about Celestial Creations?"

He angled his head, thinking. "I like that. I'll get you a nameplate."

A squawk sounded, and Tika flew over, perching on the ledge of the deck. The bird's purple beak glistened in the sun as it cocked its head at her.

She strode up to it. "You are the most beautiful parrot I've ever seen."

"Thank you. I think you're a pretty human too." The

parrot's voice reminded her of the pure vibration of a flute, both calming and piercing.

Daedriel extended his arm, and the parrot perched on it. "Cathy, I'd like to formally introduce you to my friend, Tika."

"Yes, we met the other day." Unable to resist, she reached out to pet its head, loving the softness of its feathers. "Are you male or female?"

"Male."

Cathy ogled the wonder before her. "I still can't believe I'm talking to a parrot. We have parrots here, but they're not as big or astonishing as you. They certainly don't carry on conversations the way you do."

"Thanks," Tika squawked, pride beaming from his eyes. At least, it looked like pride to her.

Though she knew it sounded bizarre, she asked Tika anyway. "Would you like to stay for dinner? I need to do some grocery shopping. I'll pick up some birdseed for you. Unless you prefer something else."

Tika flapped his wings. "Birdseed, walnuts, and vegetables. Any kind."

Daedriel's face scrunched up. "We have those at home."

Tika appeared to roll his eyes. "They've been gone since yesterday."

Cathy grinned at the odd conversation. It was a good thing the woods surrounded her property and that Daedriel was the nearest neighbor. She wouldn't know how to explain all this wonder if a stranger happened to stumble by.

Cathy shifted the strap of her purse, getting ready to go.

"Take Tika with you," Daedriel said. "After the blorvus incident, we have to be extra careful."

The hair on her arms rose from the image of the dead bird. She wasn't sure how the parrot would protect her, but she trusted Daedriel's assessment. That in itself was something she needed to evaluate. It had been a long time since she'd trusted a man so quickly.

"Okay," Cathy said. "But Tika would draw attention. Is he going to stay in my car? People would notice him, and they'll inquire."

"I have my disguise." Tika shrank in size in a flash, appearing like a little gray titmouse bird that landed in the center of her palm. "I can fit in your purse."

Cathy loved the adorable little voice. She supposed it was comforting to have an adorable bird-friend with her. She unzipped the front pouch of her purse, took out a folded piece of paper, glanced at it, and tossed it into the recycle bin.

With care, Cathy placed Tika inside the pouch. "I hope it's comfortable for you. It's not 'heavenly' leather—if there even is such a thing—but it should be soft enough."

Tika peeked his head through the zipper opening and chirped. "It's perfect."

She glanced up at Daedriel. How long had he been staring at her? His blue irises shifted as though water moved inside them.

She swallowed. "Is there anything you'd like me to pick up for you? Something you want to eat?"

"No, I'm good." He followed her out to her driveway, watching her get into her navy BMW SUV.

The ride to the grocery store would be interesting. What kind of conversation could she have with a talking bird? How much did Tika know about Daedriel? Maybe this bird wouldn't mind shedding some light on Daedriel's character.

"Let's go get you some bird food." Cathy drove out of her driveway.

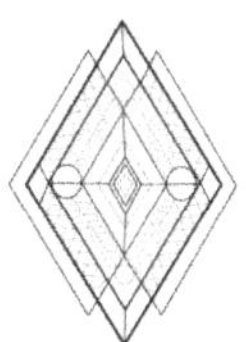

ELEVEN

Daedriel

Damaat.

Standing next to her, he sensed her body's reaction to him. The quiet passion that stirred between them was a celestial energy that wanted to create something powerful. The only thing preventing that was his will and hers.

They hadn't known each other long at all. That issue had never bothered him before. But Cathy was different. Somehow, she mattered more.

Daedriel stared after Cathy's car until it disappeared from his view. She treated Tika with so much care as though he was her own pet. Daedriel found himself wanting to share private parts of his life with her. Was it too soon?

What in the world was he doing? His desire for her had confused him, his mission, and the future he had planned for himself—one that didn't involve his heart.

Huffing out a frustrated breath, Daedriel strode back to the deck and surveyed the studio he'd built. He had put in more time and effort than necessary, but he had done that *with* purpose.

The sweat and labor allowed him to clear his mind so he could look at his situation clearly.

Were his feelings for Cathy real? It was an irrational question for someone who had lived a long time, someone who should have known better. In this rare situation, his previous experiences couldn't give him the answers he needed.

Daedriel knew his emotions, knew that passion often clouded logic. Was his desire for Cathy stemming from the center of his heart, or was it purely exterior? Was it a phase that would pass quickly? He'd encountered strong attractions before, and they had come and gone without worrying him like this.

He needed to know what was going on here. And he could only discover the truth by not using any seraph power. Magic was helpful, and he was grateful for it. But it could enhance things by throwing a veil over them, glamorizing them, making them appear *more* than what they truly were. He needed the raw truth, no matter how sharp or serrated it might be.

Daedriel didn't trust himself right now. The need to touch and protect her had risen to the fore of his thoughts. He had to take careful steps. He needed to think, to pause, so he could come to a conclusion about what he wanted with Cathy. He wasn't referring to the sexual energy hounding him. He glanced down at his jeans and cursed at the bulk pulsing in his pants.

The other reason he built her studio with labor and sweat was that a clean mental slate allowed him to evaluate his search for Rask.

When Daedriel discovered the Reverse Black Tourmaline had been stolen by one of the guards, fury had consumed him. The Celestial Realm had been deceived by one of their own. Rask had shared meals and conversations with Daedriel and his brothers. This deception was personal for Daedriel.

The mere thought of Rask infuriated him. Daedriel stalked back into the studio, shutting the door. Fury and betrayal blinded everyone, including angels. Had he missed any details that would lead him to Rask?

As Daedriel cleaned up the excess paint cans, rags, and tools, thoughts formed in his mind.

Why did Rask steal that stone? How long had he been working for the Dark Angel Agenda? Most of all, why was he on Earth?

Though Daedriel had repaired the tear in his magical cloak, it was probably too late. His seraphim energy traveled far, and someone with the ability to hone in on that energy would be able to sense him.

He placed his tools back into the duffle bag and zipped it closed. He found the T-shirt he'd tossed to the side and wiped the sweat from his body. He sniffed himself and made a disapproving hiss. He needed a shower badly. The thought of Cathy bathing with him brought a wide smile to his lips, forcing away all the irritation that had snuck up on him since she left.

He didn't like the idea of Cathy being out there by herself. Something was lurking in this city. He sensed the darkness that hovered like a whisper.

A snap sounded in the woods, and he strode out to the deck, scouring the area. Using his seraph senses, he scanned the energy. Whatever was here had masked its vibration. It knew Daedriel was here. Damaat.

Could it be Rask?

Daedriel waited a bit, concentrating on his senses. Another crack sounded, and this time his focus cut through the dense layers and zeroed in on the dark energy. In seconds, Daedriel rushed into the woods with seraph speed and chased after a pair of dark wings.

TWELVE

Cathy

She stopped at a red light and glanced at her purse. The caws from a crow that perched on a nearby tree caught Tika's attention. The little titmouse's head whipped toward the sound. The crow took off in flight somewhere.

"Have you been inside a car on Earth before?" Cathy accelerated when the lights turned green.

"Nope." Tika's voice had a cute flair to match the small body. "Daedriel doesn't always take me on his missions, but I wanted to go this time."

"Why? Did you want to visit Earth?" Cathy pulled into the parking lot of Prudent Lake Supermarket and found a parking spot away from all the other cars. She didn't want anyone seeing her talk to a bird.

"Daedriel was furious when he went after Rask. I wanted to make sure he was okay. Angels have their weaknesses too. Daedriel considered Rask a friend, as did the other seraphim. The betrayal was too much."

Cathy's heart ached for Daedriel. She turned off the engine and grabbed her purse, bringing Tika's little face closer to her. With her finger, she caressed the gray feathers on his head. "I know exactly how that feels. It's painful."

"I sensed the sadness in you the other day when you were hammering away."

Cathy recalled hearing strange squawks in the woods. "That was you?"

The titmouse nodded the only way a bird could. "I flew around, trying to get to know the area, and I heard you working. Pain gives off a vibration, but so does healing and love."

Was Tika trying to tell her something? Was there a message between the words?

"Are you trying to clue me into something, or am I just imagining things? That happens a lot, so I wouldn't be surprised."

Tika let out a few adorable chirps that sold her on having a bird for a pet. But this titmouse was not an ordinary bird. This one spoke and understood her. He came from a world beyond her grasp. Perhaps she was drawn to the novelty of this magical being. The same way she was drawn to Daedriel.

Was she attracted to him because he was an angel? She had felt a powerful attraction to him before she knew his true identity. But his otherworldly aspect fascinated her even more. He was the epitome of all the fantastical things she adored as a child. The myths and fairytales that gave a young girl the perfect escape to new worlds. To worlds that offered love and happily ever after.

"You're on a healing journey," Tika chirped. "You give off pure love. Trust and compassion too. You have a good heart. I think that's why Daedriel's drawn to you."

Her heart leaped. "He told you?" She knew he was drawn to her, but she wanted details. "What did he say?"

Tika flew out of her purse, landing on the bottom section of her steering wheel. Cathy couldn't believe she was asking a bird relationship questions that she would normally discuss with her best friend, Sydney.

She couldn't wait to catch up with Sydney and share all the incredible events she'd experienced.

Tika lifted one wing. "He feels for you in a way he's never felt before."

Joy burst in Cathy like a sunny day where everything was bright and beautiful. "He said that?"

"Not in those exact words. But I've been his friend for a long time. I know him. I sense his energy too." Tika dove back into her purse, with his head peeking out. "It's not the same kind of affection he has for me. Sexual energy from a seraph is potent. I need to get away from him when it's that strong. I like my feathers intact, thank you very much."

Cathy's face burned with embarrassment. She didn't know whether to laugh or remain serious. Having a sexual discussion with a bird was something she'd never forget. Tika spoke in a serious manner that illustrated how much Daedriel wanted her.

A knock on her window sounded, and she jumped. She glanced up at Victor's beaming face. She waved back and then held up a finger, signaling that she'd be out in a second.

Cathy checked to make sure Tika was safely hidden in her purse. She got out of the car and shut the door.

"Hi, Victor." She glanced at the cart full of groceries. "Shopping for Rosa? How's she doing?"

Victor's shoulders slumped and he released a sigh. "She didn't sleep well last night, and neither did I. She's sleeping right now, so I went out to get some food." He looked exhausted, older.

"Make sure you get enough rest too. You need to be well so you can take care of her."

Cathy made a note to inform him to take next week off too. She'd keep him on the payroll as if he didn't miss any work. Victor and Rosa had been a tremendous help to her mom and now her. Rosa and her mom used to chat about crystals and esoteric interests that Cathy loved. She considered them friends, and friends help each other out when things don't go well.

Victor nodded. "I will. Lizzi is flying in from New York tomorrow to help us."

"That's fantastic. I haven't seen her in so long. I'd love to catch up with her."

Lizzi lived with her parents before she became a famous model, sought after by designers for their fashion shows.

"I'll let her know. I won't keep you. There's a sale on asparagus, apples, and chocolate chip cookies."

"Thanks for the tip." Cathy appreciated that he remembered what she liked. She hoped Rosa would recover soon, for her sake and her husband's.

Victor got into his van, which was parked two rows behind hers, and Cathy placed one earbud into her ear. This way, she could speak to Tika if needed, and people would just assume she was on the phone.

"Victor and Rosa are a lovely couple. Rosa's sick right now, and Victor is taking on a lot of responsibilities."

"He's very worried. And he needs sleep," Tika chirped quietly.

"He does need the rest."

Cathy's attention swerved back to her plan to seduce Daedriel. She couldn't back out now. What Tika told her only hardened her resolve.

"Tika, I need your help. What kind of food does Daedriel like? Does he eat human food?"

A little beak peeked out from the zipper slit. "He can eat food from all dimensions. Food on Earth has lower vibration, so digestion is slower than food from other places. But that doesn't stop him. It doesn't stop me either. He loves chicken and stir fry vegetables."

"What about you? Stir fry vegetables too?"

"No, thanks. Just nuts, fresh vegetables, and fruits are fine with me."

With a gentle pat to her pouch, Cathy strode toward the entrance. "I'm going to make him a delicious dinner that'll have him agreeing to anything I ask."

THIRTEEN

Daedriel

He rushed into the woods, moving quietly, not wanting to startle whoever was there. The crackling sound echoed louder.

Deeper into the woods, he sensed dark energy. Something snapped, and the energy from the ground shifted. His body recalibrated itself, adjusting to the wave of darkness brewing there.

Damaat!

Daedriel made his way toward the dark vibration and stopped. Fifteen feet away, a demon from the Dark Angel Agenda waved a hand over the ground. Dark energy flowed from his hands, entering the soil in streams of tar-like liquid. Daedriel whipped out his blade of blue fire and severed the streams.

The demon whipped his attention to Daedriel. Dressed in black, he had a belt decked with weapons. Angry red veins pulsed across his forehead and down the side of his gray face. Fear and something else flashed in those dark, elongated eyes as they stared at Daedriel. The demon squinted and the gesture reminded Daedriel of the fugitive he'd been searching for.

"You can't run anymore, Rask." Daedriel narrowed his eyes at the void pitch seeping through Rask's palm. "What are you doing to the ground?"

Rask's appearance had changed from when he was a guard in the Celestial Realm. His light tan skin had turned to a crackling gray like dried mud. His cheeks had hollowed out, his blond hair replaced by a bald head from which two horns protruded.

Had he always been in disguise? Or had something happened to alter his appearance?

Energy shifted under the ground again like a quiet earthquake trying to fight off foreign intrusion. Daedriel had too many questions for Rask to kill him right away.

"What were you doing to the ground?" Daedriel repeated. "Why is the energy different?"

Rask laughed. There was something different about his eyes. Was it a struggle? Daedriel couldn't be sure.

Smiling, Rask clenched and unclenched his fists. "The Reversal Black Tourmaline is gone." His voice had changed to a rough tone.

Fury spiked in Daedriel. "What the hell did you do? Do you understand how dangerous that stone is?"

A mocking laugh escaped Rask. "I know *exactly* what it's capable of. It's why I just released it into the Aurum Grid on Earth. The ley lines are now infected, and there's nothing you can do about it."

Daedriel's fury turned to terror. "You did what?"

"The Dark Angel Agenda is gathering an army. We'll win this war, Daedriel. Why don't you join us? With your power, we can overcome the Celestial Realm and rule the Universe. Rule all the dimensions."

Daedriel had never imagined the Reversal Black Tourmaline would be used in this way. It was a dangerous weapon the dark needed. This stone collected powerful dark energy that was in the process of being alchemized. With its release, all the ancient darkness that was trapped inside that stone would grow again.

The ley lines were part of the Aurum Grid, an energy net around Earth connected to the Celestial Realm. Infecting the energy grid on Earth would indirectly infect the Celestial Realm.

Damaat! The fucking DAA was attacking his realm by attacking Earth.

The Reversal Black Tourmaline was the catalyst the demons needed to start a war on Earth. A stolen gem had become a catastrophe that would require more than Daedriel to fix.

He had more questions for Rask. Rask needed to be captured. Seraph fire heated behind Daedriel's eyes. Glaring at Rask, he shot out blue flames at a guard he once called a friend. Rask darted away swifter even than a seraph now. He had become stronger. If Rask had had this power when he first escaped, Daedriel wouldn't have been able to track him.

Too many questions popped into Daedriel's head, but he didn't have time to contemplate as a blanket of darkness rose from the ground.

"You dishonor what the Celestial Realm gave you. You betrayed us. You brought more darkness into a world where too much of it already existed. Damaat, Rask. What happened to you?"

"It had to be done," Rask said in a voice Daedriel recognized. But then it changed as though someone else was inside Rask. "It's too late for you to do anything. The Seraphim Angel Order will be destroyed. The plan is already in motion."

With that, Rask ran toward an opening in the woods,

extended a pair of bat wings, and took off into the sky. Daedriel flung out a pair of blue wings and took off after Rask. He flapped once, twice, catching up to Rask. When Rask was within his range, Daedriel shot seraph fire from his eyes, severing one of the bat wings. Rask spiraled toward the ground. Needing Rask for questioning, Daedriel caught him.

Big mistake.

A sharp blade punctured Daedriel's side, and pain bloomed along the length of his torso. Daedriel shoved Rask toward the ground, landing as best he could with the wound burning his flesh. The blood that spilled from him should have been orange like the rays of the sun, but instead, it was brown. Poison had seeped into his blood.

Rask pushed himself up from the ground, letting out a maniacal laugh. He didn't appear bothered that one of his wings was missing. Clouds of darkness surrounded them, and the smell of violence and death overwhelmed the area. The ground trembled slightly as if the infection had taken place in Earth's core.

"Join us or die." Dark clouds covered Rask and yanked him somewhere.

Infused with rage, Daedriel shot blue fire from his eyes into the dark clouds. A scream echoed. Did it belong to Rask or some other evil creature that had helped him escape?

Daedriel didn't have enough energy to go after Rask. He shouldn't have dug into his well of power for the last attack. He should have saved his energy, but he couldn't help it. The poison from the stab wound coursed in his body. He had to extract every drop of it before it crippled him.

He pressed a hand to the wound, sealing it with energy as best he could. With his last ounce of energy, he flew home.

Cathy

As she pulled into her driveway, Tika darted onto her dashboard. "He's injured."

"What do you mean?" Fear churned in Cathy's stomach.

"He's bleeding. I need to get home. Stay here."

Cathy pressed a button, opening the car window for Tika. The titmouse transformed back into the white parrot and flew off.

She stashed the perishables in the refrigerator and rushed out to the deck. What had happened while she was at the store? She wanted to check on Daedriel, but Tika's words echoed in her mind. *Stay here.* Would Tika call to update her? Did he know how to do that? Would the parrot return to let her know? What if Daedriel needed her help?

Daedriel was an angel. Who could've hurt him? Had more blorvuses returned to attack Daedriel? Goosebumps rose on her arms at the idea. Rubbing her arm, she entered the studio he'd built for her. He had gathered the miscellaneous items into a pile to be discarded. His duffle bag lay against the wall. Daedriel had been cleaning up. Something had probably distracted him and led him away from the studio.

This studio meant so much to her. He had given her a gift, a dream that turned out more beautiful than she could ever have imagined. Her heart ached, wondering if he was safe. Love and courage soared in her.

Cathy stalked over to his duffle bag, searched for the hammer he'd used earlier, and grabbed the silver handle. She rushed out of her studio and down the stairs, hammer in hand. She gripped the hammer tighter as she quickened her steps toward his house. As she moved, she glanced around her, making sure there were no blorvuses. She didn't know if it was her imagination or the adrenaline coursing through her blood, but she felt her balance off-kilter as she walked on the dirt path. Was the ground moving?

Ignoring it, she raced up his deck and pounded her fist against the back door.

When Daedriel opened it, surprise splashed on his face. "Hi. What are you doing here?" His gaze went straight to the hammer in her hand. "What are you doing with my hammer?"

She surveyed his face, down his chest, and legs. He wore a black T-shirt and gray cotton pants. He didn't appear to be injured. Had Tika been wrong?

A slew of sentences flew out of her. "I was worried about you. Tika said you were hurt. He told me to stay and wait. It drove me crazy, so I came to check on you. Are you okay? You don't look like you're hurt. What happened?"

She blew out a breath, and anxiety untangled in her.

What the hell was wrong with her? She didn't usually babble like that.

A smile formed on his face. He took the hammer from her hand, and it glowed. "Come inside."

She entered a large modern kitchen with state-of-the-art appliances, gray tiles, and metal chairs. Other than that, the kitchen was empty, as though no one lived there. Even with someone who had just moved in, she expected to see boxes of stuff. But his home appeared empty. Like he had already packed up.

Was he moving? Her heart dove to the bottom of her stomach, giving her the worst tummy ache. She clenched her stomach.

Concern flashed on his face. "Are you okay?"

"Just a stomachache." She inhaled a few breaths and released them. "Why is your home so empty? Are you moving?"

"Is that what you think?" His blue eyes darkened on her.

She was done pretending. Nodding, she said, "Yes."

"Was that the reason for the stomachache?"

She blushed at the absurdity. "Yes."

Tika appeared from nowhere and perched on the kitchen counter. "You were supposed to stay home."

Cathy flicked him an annoyed look. "And *die* of worry? I didn't know if you were coming back, and I couldn't just stand around waiting. I had to do something."

Daedriel waved his hammer as pride glinted in his eyes. "She came armed with a weapon."

Tika squawked and flew over, hovering in front of her. "Sorry. I had to make sure Daedriel was all right without putting you in danger. Darkness was looming in the area. I didn't want to frighten you."

Cathy whirled to Daedriel. "So you *were* hurt?"

He placed the hammer on the counter. "Come into my office, and I'll show you."

Tika squawked and flew into a different room.

She strode past a bathroom, two bedrooms, and a den, all of which appeared empty of life. Gray tones coated the walls.

Artwork and a splash of color would give his home some much needed vibrancy. The interior needed a facelift. He was so good at building. Why didn't he take care of the interior design too?

"Are you sure you live here?" she asked.

Daedriel laughed. "I know how it looks. I haven't had time to decorate."

He led her into a wide and open office with a panoramic view of the woods. A long gray desk anchored near the window with a brown chair. Like her desk, it was made from the Taram tree. The desk lacked a computer, books, papers, pens—all the usual accessories found in an office. There were no bookcases, no art, rugs, or lamps. Nothing.

She furrowed her eyebrows, wondering how he worked if he didn't even have a computer. He strode over to the window, glancing out into the woods. She stood beside him, studying his contemplative look. Whatever had happened while she was shopping had worried him. Stress dug into his forehead, and anxiety steeled his jaw.

Without thinking, she reached up to touch his face, wanting to soothe his stress. He turned, clutched her hand, and held it.

"Where were you hurt?" she asked. "Tika said you were bleeding."

Daedriel lifted the hem of his T-shirt. A long gash ran the length of his rib cage.

Cathy cringed as if she could feel the weapon that had punctured his side. She imagined the injury was probably worse before he had cleaned it up. A layer of medicine covered it like a transparent bandage. A smear of dried, orange blood peeked through the bandage. Was that his blood color? Or was the orange a reaction from some kind of antibiotic ointment?

"Does it hurt?" She glared at the wound, wishing it knew how she detested it. It had scarred him—her perfect man. The desire to keep him safe surged through her. She didn't understand it one bit. She'd never felt this way toward a man who could take care of himself better than her. Still, that emotion whirled within her.

From the moment they met, emotions from some deep part of her had decided to parade themselves in front of her, asking to be seen. She had to sit down and consider what was real as opposed to what was temporary. What was the truth when all the noise and confetti settled? She didn't have time for illusions.

"Not anymore." He dropped the hem of his shirt, blocking her glare at the injury. "Tika arrived just in time to help me stop the bleeding with his magic. He got my seraph wine—the Lavandula. It refueled me enough for me to start recharging myself. The poison weakened my bodily systems."

"Poison?" Terror clutched her heart, and she yanked his shirt up again. "Are you sure you're okay? Do you need a doctor? Did you take any medicine?" The questions darted out of her mouth before she realized who she was talking to. She pulled down his shirt and looked at him. "Sorry. I sometimes forget you're an angel, so you don't need the standard medicinal treatment like us humans."

"I need all of those things, just in different ways. I love that you're concerned. I'm okay, don't worry."

Was he just saying that to hide something from her? She knew that kind of reverse psychology. Gavin had coded his words, saying one thing and meaning something else. Was Daedriel trying to keep her from something he thought she couldn't handle? Was she overthinking things?

Cathy tried to imagine the state he was in. "I noticed some orange blood that dried up around your wound. Is your blood orange?"

"You're very perceptive. Angels from the SAO have blood blessed by the Celestial Sunstone, which was a gift from Source. The power of sunlight helps to protect us while we're traveling through dimensions with various energy frequencies. It allows us to adapt quickly. Angel blood is normally a dark purple."

Cathy's mind opened a little more every time she spoke to him. The vastness of the Universe astounded her.

Though the warrior standing before her embodied strength, she remembered Tika saying Daedriel had weaknesses too. What kind of weaknesses did Daedriel have? Would he share them with her?

His gaze pinned her, and her body warmed from its intensity. Desire swam in those blue irises with their gold specks that resembled tiny shards of glass bursting from the dark pupils. So much wisdom, mystery, and experience were captured in them. She wanted to dive into those deep, mysterious pools to understand every aspect of him.

"Who attacked you?" she asked in a low voice.

He arched an eyebrow slowly, a skill she didn't have. "Why do you want to know?

She didn't know why his response bothered her. Could it be the suspicion in his tone? Or was it distrust? Or was it her imagination confusing the hell out of her?

Didn't he know she cared about him? Wasn't it obvious?

Feeling awkward, she wrapped her arms around her stomach, wanting to protect herself from something she didn't know. "Well, if you're uncomfortable answering that question, that's fine with me. Now that you're well, I don't have to worry. I can leave now."

Cathy's chest tightened as she stepped away from him. He gripped her arm, whirling her back to him. Her body came flush to his, her head against his shoulder. Heat pulsed from him and wrapped itself around her like a cloak.

Was this warm energy responsible for the regenerative healing he referred to? Or was it passion radiating from him?

She looked up at him, and the same intensity still stirred in his eyes. "I have to go."

His smirk pulled into a wide grin. "No, you don't. You want to be here. I *want* you here with me." His lips were a breath away from hers.

A citrus scent mixed with something unfamiliar yet enticing threatened to seduce her all over again. She inched closer for a better sniff. She loved that masculine and mysterious scent.

"I want to hear you say it," he said.

"Hear me say what?" Cathy knew what he meant. He wanted confirmation of her feelings for him. He wanted to know if this "thing" between them was real.

Was it real? The way her body melted against him agreed. The way her heart raced every time she neared him confirmed it. The only thing missing was her spoken acknowledgment to him.

She swallowed the lump that suddenly formed in her throat, preventing her from speaking. Why was she afraid to acknowledge her feelings for him? Past mistakes didn't make a present moment wrong. A bad relationship shouldn't ruin her outlook on all relationships. One bad man didn't mean they were all bad. She knew that; yet doubt had a way of making itself appear bigger than it really was.

For some reason, the image of her working on her back deck flashed into her vision. She had removed a rusty nail that hadn't supported the deck and replaced it with a shiny, new one. Like the deck, she'd been rebuilding herself all this time, one nail at a time.

There was nothing to fear but the unknown. That was her crutch. What if he didn't feel the same way? What if he just wanted something temporary while he was here on Earth? Eventually, he'd return to where he came from, leaving her behind. That thought was too much for her to bear. Her mom had recently left her, and she didn't know if she could handle another crack in her heart.

But Cathy was a businesswoman who understood the rewards of risks. Sometimes, she had to take them regardless of what the facts were. Sometimes, intuition was enough. For today, she followed her instincts.

Daedriel's bulge throbbed against his cotton pants, and heat burst in her core. She knew she had to be candid with him.

He wrapped both arms around her, caging her in an embrace with no escape, not that she wanted to. "Why do you want to know who attacked me?"

His eyes bore into hers, wanting the truth. In his eyes, she saw a woman who also wanted the truth.

"Because I care about you. I don't know why I care so much, so soon. It makes no sense to me." She exhaled slowly. "I tried dissecting it, making up excuses, but everything came down to one simple fact: I'm very attracted to you. And I care about you in a way I can't explain. Does that answer your question?"

His eyes danced. "I feel the same way about you. Hearing you say those words just escalated my healing."

Daedriel lifted his shirt again, revealing the wound that had faded significantly from minutes ago.

Astounded and delighted, she gawked at his skin's healing ability. Sparkles hovered around the scar as new layers of skin formed. The process fascinated her.

"How is that possible?" she asked.

"Loving energy enhances my power. The truer it is, the stronger my energy becomes. I've never felt this kind of force before. The acceleration of this healing comes from a love that's rare, Cathy."

Her heart jumped. Had she helped him to heal by simply admitting what was in her heart?

Daedriel lowered his lips to hers, and she sagged against

him. His strong arms held her tightly. His lips were firm and smooth, tantalizing her. She moaned, and his tongue slipped in, meeting hers. She tasted citrus mixed with some kind of wine that made her crave more. Her hand gripped his shirt, pulling him closer if that was even possible. His hand cupped the back of her neck, massaging it. She pressed her hip into him, and he growled.

He broke the kiss, and his lips ghosted over her cheek to nibble on her earlobe. "I want you, but not tonight."

"I want you too," she said. "But I want you *well* more." She placed a gentle hand over his injury.

"That wouldn't stop me from performing. Nothing can stop *those* needs." His eyes glinted with amusement. "But first, I want to show you all of me. I know you have questions, so let's get to know each other, okay?"

She'd love nothing more and started with the first question. "Where is your furniture? I was expecting to see artistic and creative designs all over the house, but the only thing I see is your desk, which looks like it's made from the Taram tree too."

"It is." He glanced at the desk and back to her. "Let's celebrate tonight. I need to grab a bottle of wine for you. Do you want to try some celestial wine?"

Was that what she'd tasted on his lips? "Absolutely."

Daedriel laughed, looking more handsome than ever. "I'll be right back."

FIFTEEN

Daedriel

As he headed to the kitchen, Daedriel couldn't stop smiling. There was no going back for Daedriel from the Seraphim Angel Order. He had fallen for a human, a woman who had the power to affect him like no one else. He placed a hand over his racing heart, feeling something shift inside him.

For the first time in his life, he was beginning to feel like he had found a home for himself. He had a feeling Cathy was his home, where his heart wanted to be. Was that why he'd been instantly attracted to her?

When Cathy expressed her feelings to Daedriel, a beam of truth shot into his heart. The honesty of it, the beauty of it, touched his heart in a magnificent way. This rare activation also zapped his blood like a new wave of circuitry had entered him, giving him something he'd never had before. While he kissed her, he felt his blood coursing through his body and pooling around his wound, healing him.

Daedriel lifted his shirt, reviewing his wound as it faded

rapidly. He opened the wine cabinet and grabbed a bottle of his Lavandula wine and two gold wine glasses. He'd never shared this wine with a human before. Did Cathy like wine? He wanted to know everything about her.

Moreover, he wanted her. It had taken all of his willpower not to take her in his office, on his desk. The sexual tension was like a huge snake wrapped around them, but he wanted to make sure Cathy knew him before she decided if she wanted to love him.

The first step was to show her his sanctuary, his most private place.

SIXTEEN

Cathy

Daedriel came back with a bottle of wine and wine glasses. He handed her the wine glasses while he popped the cork. He poured a dark blue liquid into each wine glass. Tiny stars sparkled around it.

Cathy lifted the rim and sniffed a light citrus scent. "What kind of wine is this? What's it made from?"

"It's from the Lavandula grapes." He opened his palm, and a grape appeared. "Try it."

Her lips parted, and he fed her a grape. A combination of sweet, tangy, and citrus flavors burst in her mouth. "It's delicious."

"You can only get this fruit here in my private collection and the Celestial Realm. Try the wine. Savor the flavor."

Cathy knew how to enjoy a nice glass of wine. She let the wine glide over her tongue, along her cheek, allowing some air to get in. Aeration allowed the taste to linger in the mouth. "This is an exceptional wine." She'd just tasted a bit of heaven.

Grinning, he said, "Let's get to why we're here. We can have more wine later." He took her wine glass and placed it on the desk next to his.

Daedriel faced the opposite wall, and with his free hand, he waved out a force of energy that brushed against her skin. A veil pulled away like a curtain, revealing an enormous arched doorway into another world. Soft lights burst through the open doorway.

"What do you want to know about me?" he asked. "What would you like to see first?"

"Show me your home. Where do you live? Where do you come from?"

"Let's go then."

Cathy stepped into the doorway and entered a massive room with a stone floor. Gray stone walls surrounded the room, with a few slats jutting out like shelves. Miniatures of castles and architectural structures sat on the shelves. Some of them looked like tiny replicas of the building images he'd sent her.

The ceiling in his home was also made from raw stones in shades of gray and brown. Soft lights emanated from the slits in the ceiling, and slim vertical lamps on the walls illuminated the space. Three brown couches sat in one corner of the room with a circular blue coffee table at the center. On the other side was a floating bed that overlooked a window with its curtains drawn. A modern kitchen with a stove and refrigerator looked untouched. A circular dining table had four chairs. To her left was a room full of logs and branches from the Taram tree. That was probably where he'd gotten the wood to create her office desk.

The chirps of birds echoed, and a burst of fresh air blew in from somewhere.

"Is this an angel's bachelor pad?"

Daedriel lifted a shoulder. "Something like that."

"It's very neat and clean."

"That's because I don't come here that often. Been too busy."

He led her around the corner, down a wide hallway filled with trees and plants. A small white parrot that looked like Tika flew onto his shoulder and chirped. "Greetings, Dae."

"Hi, Cici," Daedriel replied. "This is my friend, Cathy."

"Hi, Cathy." Cici flew over to Cathy's arm.

"Nice to meet you," Cathy replied. Cici's chirp sounded like a giggle as she flew away, joining other birds in various sizes and colors.

"Is that Tika's relative?" she asked, gawking after the bird with the cutest voice she'd ever heard.

"No. Same species. We saved Cici and Kiki from hungry predators a few years ago. The sisters have lived here ever since."

A blue cat-like animal with a tail that looked like a tree branch ran past her, chasing some kind of chipmunk-looking creature. "You have a zoo here."

"That's what my brothers said the last time they came to visit. They drop off stray animals here because my home is set up with food and water. The animals know what to do even when I'm not here. They also know what *not* to do."

The tone had Cathy looking around for random animal poop. "You have well-disciplined animals. Do they all talk?"

"Most of them."

"Wow." A thought occurred to her. "How many languages can you speak? Is there some kind of celestial language that all beings can understand?"

"I can speak any language. They are just sounds with a specific kind of frequency. There is the universal language that I speak with other beings from various realms."

Cathy felt like she'd been living under a rock. There was a

whole new world she didn't know about. It was so extraordinary that she was afraid everything was a dream, including the beautiful man giving her a tour of his home.

Did he realize that by showing her his space, she was seeing other parts of him that made her want him even more? He was an angel warrior who took in stray animals.

They arrived at a platform that overlooked a magnificent landscape. The infinite colorful skyline seemed to go on and on. The light illuminating the ethereal area came from everywhere. She didn't see the sun, but lights radiated from all over. Massive mountains loomed like ancient gods in the distance. A few smaller mountains suspended in the air like floating islands. Plants and flowers created colorful splashes on the mountainside. Her body relaxed from the serenity. She took in a deep breath, and the air quality revitalized her lungs. Her body shuddered from the jolt of fresh air that hinted of honeysuckle.

Orbs of light in various sizes faded in and out like moons dotting the endless horizon. As she stared at the images, a few orbs emerged with clarity as planets or moons. Some appeared close by, while others spread out into the incredible expansion.

She glanced back, looking at the wide opening she'd emerged through. "Your studio is a cave?"

He nodded. "Inside a sacred mountain. I chose this spot when I discovered it by accident a long time ago."

"Is this part of the Celestial Realm?" she asked, eyeing the yellow bird that flew past her leaving a trail of blue starlight glowing brightly.

"No, it's not. It's a sacred pocket in the twelfth-dimensional matrix. I found it, resonated with its energy, and made it my own. There are many undiscovered sanctuaries out there, and I was lucky to have stumbled on this one."

"It's your slice of heaven."

"It is." He smiled. "I brought in random plants and animals

whenever I could. Over time, this place flourished with life. It's sacred to me, and I don't come here as much as I should. Just a few visits here and there."

"Why not?"

He looked out into the distance. "Because of what I do. I brush against darkness every day. I don't want to taint this place, you know?"

Cathy understood more than he knew. To her, this exquisite place was the closest thing to a tangible heaven. She wouldn't want to bring any ugly residue into it either.

Her heart skipped a beat, knowing she was standing in a place that was precious to him. "Did you break your own rule by bringing me here?"

He met her eyes, and a smile formed on his lips. "I break the rules all the time. I can adapt to changes, and you're a life-changing event for me. Also, there are no negative vibrations from you."

This was a monumental moment for both of them and what they meant to each other. Their relationship wasn't just a physical attraction. This was something beyond that—something sacred.

Cathy glanced around, trying to get a view of the mountain she stood on, but the area was covered with plants and clouds. He led her further out to the platform where she got a closer view of the glowing globes. Her heart raced, and warmth brushed against her cheek, reminding her of that special night when she was six years old, looking up at the moon for answers. Though at that time, she didn't know she was searching for anything. She was just a child mesmerized by the beauty of the moon and the lore it possessed. The moon was where she turned when she needed comfort.

She looked at Daedriel as an epiphany surfaced. The moon

was with her when her father abandoned his family. Now, the moon brought her a man—an angel—who gave her hope again.

The warmth on her cheek traveled down her neck as her eyes landed on a familiar globe. "Is that Earth's moon?"

"Yes."

She couldn't believe it. "So those orbs are all moons?"

He nodded. "I'm fond of moons. Most seraphim have their own sanctuaries. This is mine." He jerked a finger back to the plants and animals and gestured to the glowing orbs. "I allow things I want to see to exist here. You're the first woman to be here."

She sucked in a breath, and her heart thudded. "First human woman?" She was certain he'd brought other women to his home before.

"First female... ever." He pulled out two cushioned chairs from somewhere. "Have a seat." He sat down and faced her. "Like you, I feel strongly about us. I want you to *see* me. Take a look at this."

A huge cloud appeared before her, and images began to form in it like a movie screen. But before she knew it, she and Daedriel were transported into the cloud, into the movie. As she stood inside the action like a virtual reality, her body absorbed the clang of weapons and scents of blood and death. The sight of Daedriel with his majestic blue wings gripped her. He was glorious and powerful, a mighty contrast to the horrific monsters he was battling. Fear gnawed at her as a beast slammed a fist into his stomach. Daedriel used a sword with blue flames and cleaved the monster in two. Embers floated around as the flames devoured the beast. More beasts arrived from out of nowhere and attacked Daedriel, but he killed each one of them. Blood covered his face and body. The violence and gore of the scenes made her nauseous.

A monster appeared inches from Cathy, and she flinched with a scream.

Beside her, Daedriel wrapped an arm around her trembling body, pulling her close. "They can't hurt you. I promise."

His touch calmed her, but she jumped when a sharp weapon landed inches away from her feet. A whiff of rotten stench churned her stomach, and she turned into his chest. The metallic smell of blood, the heaviness of death, and the chill of evil stabbed at her senses, making everything so real. She never thought she could smell or sense evil, but at this moment, they overwhelmed her. She felt the malice and darkness seep into her skin, biting at her slowly. Tears welled in her eyes because she knew this was what Daedriel endured. This was what he felt every time he went to battle. She tightened her arms around him, wanting to protect him from all the ugliness.

A new battle scene took over, showing Daedriel fighting angels with dark wings and horned demons with fangs and tails. His brothers, who possessed massive wings in various colors, assisted him. Daedriel's flaming sword demolished nightmarish creatures that crawled out of holes in the ground. He eradicated swarms of blorvuses larger and scarier than the bird she'd encountered in her backyard.

Powerful monsters needed powerful angels to fight them. Scene after scene, Daedriel and his brothers killed so many evil creatures. Daedriel looked exhausted, even during the victories. Violence, death, and desolation clung to him like ragged clothing that wouldn't fall off.

With so many atrocities and so much heaviness attached to him, she wondered if he could shake off all that darkness. Could his sanctuary heal him? Could it give him the love and peace he deserved?

She slid him a glance. In his eyes, she witnessed a longing for something besides violence, death, and desolation. She wanted to give him what he lacked. He had immortality, but was it worth it if it was just filled with unyielding darkness?

Tears spilled over. She couldn't stop the flow of emotion warring inside her. Immediately, the scenes stopped, and the cloud disappeared.

Daedriel wiped the tears from her eyes with his thumb, a gentle act he'd done before. "I'm sorry. I shouldn't have—"

"No. Don't be. I'm glad you showed me these parts of your life. Now I understand your important responsibilities. You're *needed* to fight the darkness. But it comes at a price, and my heart aches for you. I didn't know there was so much fighting going on outside of my small world." His hand brushed her back, and the warmth of him calmed her emotion. "You deserve love, peace, and so much more."

He kissed the top of her head. "You gave me that spark of hope again, Cathy. You're the opposite of the dark. You're the light I've been waiting for. We have something in common."

She veered back to look at him. "What do you mean?"

He pointed to the sky which had shifted to a darker blue and purple with its twinkling stars. "I sensed your love for the moon. There's moon energy around you. You have a unique connection to it. You believe in the stories associated with it, like the Moon Goddess. Stories are magical because they have the power to make you believe, and belief makes things real. My previous responsibility before I joined the Seraphim Angel Order was to monitor moon frequency. Everything needs balance to survive in a healthy way."

Cathy couldn't help but wonder if the Moon Goddess had heard her prayers from years ago. Was Daedriel the love she'd been waiting for? Her heart hammered a loud "yes!" He had been a moon guardian, and she had been fascinated with the moon ever since she was a child. Not only that, but she also sensed its presence during pivotal moments in her life.

"What is the real story behind Earth's moon? Is there a goddess or fairy up there?" she asked.

"Earth's moon isn't an organic moon," he began. "It wasn't a natural part of Earth's orbit. Earth is a fertile planet with tons of resources like water and gold. Some referred to it as the Living Library because it stores sacred codes and information from various life forms. Before humans began populating this planet, there were beings that wanted to experiment on this fertile land. They wanted to control it. So they brought in a moon, set up a base *inside* the moon, transforming it into a satellite that sent out beams of energy to control the frequency around Earth."

Cathy tried to grasp what he was telling her. It was so bizarre, so incredible that she didn't know how to respond. The only thing that came to her mind was, "Who are these beings?"

"There are many powerful entities out there. Aliens, angels, creatures from all over who yearned for power. So when they discovered a gem like Earth, they all wanted it. But you see, when they began using the moon as a 'computer' to control what happened on Earth, they began to play with free will. And that goes against the law of the Universe."

"Wait a second, you're telling me there are beings inside the moon?"

"Most of them have evacuated because the warriors of light have pushed them out. There are divine angels, goddesses, elven warriors, dragons, and other positive entities circling the moon to protect it. Perhaps one of them has shown itself to humans, and that was how legends began."

"So there's a dark side to the moon, literally and figuratively," she said as she tried to envision someone living inside the moon. Her mind had been stretched beyond belief with this information.

Daedriel gave a slow nod. "But the light shines on it too, and that's when you have the full moon. There are warriors up there, still trying to extract whatever is still inside. But the frequency the moon emits is manageable now. I don't see any hazardous energy coming it."

That settled her nerves. In the distance, a dull moon caught her attention. "What happened to that one over there? Is that an inorganic moon too?"

"No, that was a natural moon, but it's lifeless now. We can check out Oriss. Do you want to fly with me?"

A thrill rushed through her. "I'd love to."

SEVENTEEN

Daedriel

Cathy's eyes gleamed. "I finally get to see your wings."

"You're curious about that?" He loved knowing she wanted to see all aspects of him.

"Of course!" Her eyes widened. "I've never seen an angel before. From the cloud movie, I know you have impressive blue wings. I only saw one set though. You said you have six wings. *Show me.*"

The excitement in her voice made him smile. "Yes, ma'am."

Grinning, she stepped back, giving him room. With his mind, Daedriel connected to his wings, telling them to emerge slowly. Daedriel wanted Cathy to see the process. He'd never really paid attention to the emergence of his wings. They had always been part of him, and he took that for granted.

At this moment, he gave them his attention. His shoulder blades hardened, and the deltoids and trapezius muscles on his back strengthened. He zeroed in on the sensation as the top set of wings broke through his skin, expanding to full size. His shoulder joints, collar bones, and humeri increased power to uphold the massive weight. The shoulder blades on both sides increased in width and length to accommodate two more sets of wings, which emerged below the top set.

Cathy studied him with keen interest. Her eyes glittered with wonder. He'd never been *admired* like that. He felt like a masterpiece standing before her.

The six wings flapped behind him, creating a gentle breeze that blew Cathy's black hair around. With awe, she walked up to him, brushed her fingers down his blue feathers.

"They're soft, yet they look like metal," she said. Her fingers lovingly caressed the vanes of his feathers, making him yearn for her touch on other parts of his body. His arousal thickened, and he cursed under his breath. This wasn't the time for sexual needs. He forced himself to think of things that would push sexual desires from his mind.

A feather fell from his wing and floated down into her palm. She flicked him a glance and smiled. "It fell for me."

He read between the lines. "It did."

Her expression softened as she understood his reply. "May I have this?"

Daedriel blinked at the odd question no one had ever asked him. "Sure. What are you going to do with it?"

"Would it offend you if I used it like one of those old quill pens? I'd like to dip it in ink and draw with it."

Daedriel didn't expect that at all. "No offense taken. I'm curious what you'll draw. I want to see it."

"When I'm done, I'll show it to you." She touched his biceps and squeezed. "I noticed your arms jerked a bit when the wings expanded. Do your bones thicken to support all this weight?"

"I love how perceptive you are. All the bones and muscles

on my shoulders, arms, and back increase in strength." He clutched her hand. "Fly with me."

"Been waiting for you to say that. What do I do?"

"Hold on to me."

EIGHTEEN

Cathy

Daedriel's arm wrapped around her waist, pulling her flush to his body. A pair of wings beat, taking them into the air. He flapped once and then twice, letting them glide slowly. The bottom wings supported her legs like an embrace, making her feel safe. She wasn't afraid of heights, but she would never go skydiving. The idea of being exposed in the open space with no safety net terrified her, but at this moment, she had no fear. She glanced below her, but all she saw were twinkling stars and other glowing orbs. The top set of wings supported her arms.

They approached the dull moon, landing gracefully on the cracked surface. Daedriel folded the wings on his back and walked around the area that had no life left. No trees, no water, no animals. Nothing.

For some reason, sadness overwhelmed her. A longing she didn't understand surrounded her, as though she sensed the demise woven around this moon. The ground quaked a little, then stopped.

"What was that?"

"A small moonquake." Daedriel, with his gorgeous blue wings, was a brilliant contrast to the dull area. "The life on Oriss died when its water planet, Zintaka, dried up. This moon used to have crystalline clear water on it. It's tied to its home planet like a child to its mother. When Zintaka died, it died too."

She sensed the regrets in his voice. "What happened?"

"My brothers and I were too late to help the Zintakans. Other races came to destroy their home. They're powerful beings with a connection to water. Their species have spread to different planets and other realms now. They don't have a home to come back to." He bent down and touched the dry sand. "I brought the moon back to my place to remind me why I continue to fight the dark. If I don't, all the worlds will be like this."

A thought occurred to her. "Is there any way to bring the planet back to life? Or this moon back to its original state?"

He rose and stood in front of her. "I don't know. There are so many lifeless moons and planets out there in the Universe. I had friends from Zintaka, so I brought their moon back to remember them. But there are thousands of dead moons out there. If there is a way, I haven't heard of it. Truth is, I never had the time to find out. I was always trying to keep up with the battles."

Something about Oriss touched her. Maybe it was because it was linked to Daedriel. She didn't like the sorrow on his face. Or maybe it was because of her fondness for Earth's moon. It offered light and hope to those who looked up to it. She was used to seeing the glowing orb in the sky and didn't know how she would feel if she never saw it again.

"You're on Earth because you don't want the darkness to consume my home. I'll help you find the monster responsible for your injuries." She twisted her lips. "I'd appreciate it if you could teach me how to use that hammer of yours. When you held it, it glowed, moved, and did stuff. But when I held it, nothing happened."

He laughed, and the beautiful sound gave life to this lifeless terrain. "You want to learn how to use that hammer to help me fight Rask?"

She narrowed her eyes. "Why not?"

"Sure, I'll show you how to use it. Want a tour of the sky before bedtime?"

"You know, I had a well-thought-out plan to cook you an amazing dinner and then seduce you. But the day spiraled out of control."

Amusement glinted in his eyes. "*Really?* I'll be over tomorrow."

Daedriel held Cathy with his strong arm and divine wings. He glided toward three orbs that created an arch of energy similar to the doorway in his office. As he passed through the magical portal out of his sanctuary, a wave of peace brushed against her like a blessing. The next second, they flew down the East Coast of the United States of America. As he showed her the beauty of the land and sea, love swelled in her heart. She pressed her face into the crook of his neck, took in the scent of him, and admitted something to herself. She was in love with an angel with blue wings. That admission was a gentle feather, caressing and tickling her soul.

She giggled as her feet skimmed the waters of the Atlantic Ocean and the peaks of the Appalachian Mountains. When he sailed her close to the moon, her heart hammered at its quiet beauty.

Don't you dare emit negative vibrations to Earth, she told whoever was still inside the moon.

Cathy swung her attention to the entities protecting the

moon. She'd always believed there was a Moon Goddess. Cathy could ask her for a wish on the day of the full moon, which was in two days.

An idea popped into her mind. She knew what she could make Daedriel.

NINETEEN

Daedriel

The next afternoon, Daedriel brought in furniture from the storage in his sanctuary and filled his home and walls with comfortable chairs, pillows, and art he'd collected over the years. He'd never felt the need to take them out to decorate his temporary home. Because after he apprehended Rask, he'd move on to another mission, and his new "home" would be where the responsibility took him.

Because of Cathy, his outlook had changed. She had inspired him to update his home, to make it comfortable and colorful for when she visited. Before Cathy, his mission had been simple but tiresome. He'd chased after the darkness to eliminate it. But now, he had *more* to fight for. He had Cathy to protect. He'd never imagined his purpose would alter for anyone. Cathy gave him more than a purpose—she gave him the spark to become a better seraph.

Tika noticed the change in Daedriel and wouldn't stop talking. The bird squawked as he perched on the new tables, flew to the chairs, studied the floor lamps, and darted over to the art figurines, and so on. They weren't "new" items, but they had never been displayed in any of his homes.

"You should've done this from the beginning!" Tika's beak clicked. "Love is the only thing that has the power to change you." It wasn't a question but a statement that hit the center of his heart. "I'm hungry. See you later."

The parrot flew back into his room, and Daedriel entered his office, closing the door to ponder on that topic—love.

Last night when he showed Cathy the sky, the mountains, and the ocean, he was showing her the world through his eyes. Through the beauty and power of flight, he could take her to places she'd never been before. From her wonderful sighs and gasps, he knew he'd given her something she'd remember forever.

But that delight wasn't just for her. She gave him something too. He'd never explored the world with a woman clutched to his body. It was intimate, sexual. It was like a sacred bond between two souls that belonged together. He loved the way her body molded to his during the flight. How his wings cupped her body, allowing her to feel protected while they soared over the landscape.

At that moment, an outline of the diamond light formed in his heart, illuminating in his mind's eye. Cathy had activated the diamond-shaped crystal inside a seraph's heart. He'd heard about it, but none of his brothers had spoken about the activation.

Its presence was profound in the most subtle way. It wasn't the lightning bolt of energy he expected. It was more of a gentle drop of dew that fell onto his chest, seeped into his skin, and seeded in his heart. The delicate process etched in his mind like poetry as soon as he left his sanctuary. He had felt a shift in his heart when he first met her, but it was during the shared flight when he realized what was happening inside him. He heard her heartbeat next to his, and the sound of it was like a key, unlocking other parts of him. He was no poet—had no time for such things—which was why he deemed this entire experience as a divine phenomenon. He glanced out the window toward the sky, wondering if Source had constructed this path for him.

Daedriel had only met Source twice, in the form of supreme light. The first time was when the Dark Angel Agenda killed his parents. A ball of light had pulsed in front of Daedriel. The light spoke in a male voice, asking Daedriel to join the Seraphim Angel Order. The presence of Source eased his grief, allowing him to move forward quicker than he anticipated.

Daedriel's second experience with Source was during a meeting with his brothers. At that time, the voice was female. He concluded that this supreme energy was both male and female, god and goddess. Did it matter to him? No. The entire Universe was so complex, even he often found himself confused, wondering why Source couldn't just eliminate the darkness all at once. That would have saved time, pain, and bloodshed.

He did ask that question but more diplomatically. The answer he received wasn't as clear as it should have been.

There's a plan behind the scenes woven with lessons, growth, and wisdom. All of these things must move in accordance with free will. They are part of the evolution for all organisms, even you, seraph. Life is a beautiful journey for everyone and everything. And I need your help to preserve that beauty.

Daedriel always knew that his purpose was to preserve that which was good. But Cathy had opened him to a profound understanding of his existence. He had never felt so alive than when he was with her. And because of that potent emotion—that *love*—he comprehended the "beauty" of what Source meant. The definition of that word would be different for everyone. And there lay the true wisdom of the Universe.

From what he'd witnessed in his lifetime, he knew that "gods" and "heroes" hurt other beings, angels, creatures, and people. The ones who called themselves "gods" weren't true aspects of the divine source because the genuine Source was an energetic being watching the "evolution" play out without interfering with the flow of free will.

These so-called "gods" gave themselves a name that placed them on a pedestal. They didn't win wars by striking down a single villain. Sometimes, innocent lives fell victim to the actions of those deemed as "gods" and "heroes." There were consequences to everything, cause and effect.

Daedriel didn't want to be in either category. He just wanted to eliminate as much darkness as he could and *preserve* the beauty of life. He wanted to remember his parents and the love they had for him. Otherwise, what was the purpose of living?

Daedriel's heart hammered, memorizing the rhythm of Cathy's heartbeat. That was how he knew he'd fallen in love with her. It shocked him because he thought love required more time to develop. But he stopped contemplating and just accepted this sacred emotion in him.

Sighing, he dropped into his office chair. How did Cathy feel about him? The attraction was there—it pulsed between them. But did she feel something more than the physical attraction?

He wanted to know, but he didn't want to frighten her. He'd give her all the time she needed. He had all the time in the world. Had she thought about his immortality? Did it bother her? Mortality was a topic they had to discuss at a later time.

Daedriel steered his focus back to Rask. Before bed last

night, he had used his phone and sent a signal to Eraton, one of his brothers, for assistance.

A beat of the wing sounded outside of his office. Sensing his brother's arrival, Daedriel waved his hand, and the sliding door opened. Eraton folded his iridescent orange wings on his back and entered through the door. He wore black pants and a textured white shirt.

Daedriel rose from his chair, nodded, rounded his desk, tapping forearm to forearm with his brother. "That was fast. What dimension did you come from?"

With a swoosh, Eraton's wings disappeared from his back. "From the ninth dimension. I had an investigation that ended early, so that freed me up." He glanced around the room. "This office looks cozy, which isn't you. I was expecting a cold, empty room. What happened here? Was this place pre-furnished?" He took a seat in one of the two chairs Daedriel had placed in front of his desk.

"I just wanted to decorate my office. What's wrong with that? I knew you were coming, so I wanted something for you to put your ass in."

Eraton roared with laughter. "Now that's the biggest seraph lie I've ever heard. You don't care what happens to my ass. It's creepy that you're even thinking about my ass."

"Stop the ass talk." Daedriel rolled his eyes. He cursed himself for being careless with his choice of words. Eraton appeared to be clinging to it for some damn reason.

"I didn't start the conversation." Eraton crossed his legs. "After we get the serious discussion out of the way, I'm going to hound you about what happened here." He cocked his head, and a smirk curved onto his lips. "You can't hide your energy, brother."

Seraphim could sense each other's energy better than other angels. Daedriel and Eraton had fought battles together, so there was a special bond that spanned hundreds of years. The Seraphim Angel Order portrayed the strongest bond of any brotherhood he'd encountered. Their shared experiences in warfare and violence strengthened their friendship. These angels would give their life for him and he for theirs.

"If you have any brain cells left after we discuss the issues with the Aurum Grid, I'll think about sharing some personal details with you." Daedriel wasn't sure where to begin. He had arrived on Earth with one task, one priority: apprehend Rask and retrieve the Reversal Black Tourmaline. So far, he'd failed.

Eraton tapped his head. "You always said I have a big head. I've got plenty of brain cells, don't you worry. So what's wrong with the Aurum Grid?"

"Rask destroyed the Reversal Black Tourmaline and poured it into the Earth. The darkness shook the ground that day. I know something's changed in the Aurum Grid. Rask is more powerful here. Maybe he's drawing in dark energy."

"I wouldn't be surprised if the DAA gave him a boost. How many fallen angels and other beings have we killed? Too many." Eraton's amber eyes hardened. "We've lost brothers and sisters to The Dark Angel Agenda. Dark energy is growing every day. I sensed it in the ninth dimension as well. They're everywhere."

The Seraphim Angel Order had been trying to figure out who led the DAA. As far as Daedriel knew, it was someone powerful enough to mask his or her energy from the seraphim. That was a huge task for another day that required all seraphim and celestial beings to investigate. For now, Daedriel focused on what was in front of him.

"Can you get me the status of the Aurum Grid? A copy of the energetic map would be fantastic. I would make a trip back to the Celestial Realm, but I fear that the moment I leave, something drastic would happen here." He felt that in his heart. "The reception from here isn't clear enough for me to review the grid. At least not an accurate one."

"Have you tried contacting the Cartographer? She can get you any current map you need."

Daedriel had thought about that, but he didn't want to bother the wise woman who was so much more to him, the seraphim, and other celestial beings, than a mapmaker. "I don't want to interrupt her. You know how busy she is always with her school and students. This is something we can take care of."

Sighing, Eraton said, "She should retire. The Oracle Academy has enough teachers. Anyway, I'll head back now and return tomorrow."

"Excellent. Thanks." Daedriel didn't share with Eraton that he didn't want to leave Cathy unattended, *unprotected*. With the diamond light in his heart, his enemies would know his weakness. Cathy wouldn't stand a chance if Rask came at her the way he did with Daedriel.

Eraton pushed up from his chair. "It's the full moon tomorrow. The energy is potent for us on the side where the light shines. The dark side is where evil will gather and intensify. I bet Rask will show himself somehow. He's going to feed from the dark side."

Smiling, Daedriel stood up. "That was my hope. The Aurum Grid can show me exactly what the Reversal Black Tourmaline did to the Earth. From there, we can determine what Rask has been up to and locate him."

"We can scour this area for Rask. With two of us, we can find him faster," Daedriel said.

"I'm game for hunting." Eraton walked around the office. "So, who's the woman?"

Daedriel rounded his desk and leaned against it, crossing his arms. "What makes you think it's a woman?"

Eraton offered a half-smile. "How long have I known you?

You're radiating lust, passion, and power. They're choking me." He made a choking sound.

Brothers could be so annoying, Daedriel thought, but he loved them nonetheless.

"If you keep asking, I'll choke you myself."

"You should be happy I'm asking. I'm just helping you release some of that sexual tension."

Admitting the truth to Eraton would make Daedriel's emotions official.

Daedriel uncrossed his arms and braced his hands on the edge of his desk. "I'm in love, you piece of shit."

"Now, that's no way to talk to a seraph." Eraton laughed. "I want to meet her."

It would mean the world to Daedriel for his brothers to meet Cathy. "Get me the information, and I'll introduce you. Now go!" He had work to do before his dinner date with Cathy later in the evening.

"I don't report to you, Dae. But since you're in *looove*, I'll let it slide."

"Just wait until it's your turn, asshole."

Eraton snorted. "I prefer my single lifestyle."

That was what Daedriel had said to himself before he met the woman who changed everything for him.

After Eraton left, Daedriel texted Cathy, informing her when he'd be over for dinner. Was she still going to seduce him? A smile curved his lips and remained there until he sensed a wave of dark energy and went to check it out.

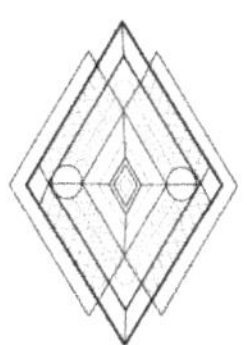

TWENTY

Cathy

Hope was something hard to reclaim, but Daedriel offered that with his presence. She'd never felt more hopeful. It had even given her an idea for her greeting card collection. She couldn't wait to start on the prototypes. But first, she had to take care of today's agenda.

On top of her to-do list was dinner for Daedriel—her warrior angel.

Cathy spent the morning at the Asian supermarket, gathering last-minute ingredients for mooncakes and grabbed a pack of longevity noodles. In the past, she'd shared a special tradition of making mooncakes with her mom. But after she passed, Cathy hadn't been in the mood. However, this new spark in her life had inspired her to do what she loved again.

She canceled the mooncake order she had placed a few days ago and replaced it with an order of dry shiitake mushrooms. The store owner was her mom's friend, so she wanted to support them in any way she could.

For this year's Mid-Autumn Festival, Cathy was going to start a new tradition. She was making mooncakes for Daedriel. She wouldn't be making the traditional mooncakes with the salted egg yolks and shiny, golden brown exterior. Those were reserved for her mom.

Cathy would be making the non-traditional snow skin mooncakes with purple sweet potato filling and translucent mochi skin. She'd made it before with her mom's guidance and loved how they were steamed rather than baked.

Cathy wanted to give Daedriel something that came from her heart. Tomorrow was the August Full Moon on the lunar calendar, and she sensed the magic of it. She wanted to acknowledge the Moon Goddess for hearing her prayer all those years ago about her request for true love.

She could see Daedriel's affection for her in his eyes. Something truly beautiful had blossomed between them, and she thanked the Moon Goddess for him.

When Cathy arrived home, she set out the purple sweet potatoes, glutinous rice flour, coconut cream, coconut milk, and condensed milk and got to work. After all the steaming, kneading, rolling, and shaping, she took out her circle mold and formed a dozen snow skin mooncakes. The simple emblem on the surface gave her room to personalize the cakes for Daedriel.

Cathy placed four mooncakes in a box and set it aside for Sydney. She packed another four to give to Victor and Rosa before placing two mooncakes on a silver plate and dedicating them to her mom. She moved the plate over to the windowsill, so that the moon could see them—so that her mom could see them wherever she was.

Emotions swelled in her as she looked at the beautiful cakes. They were a reminder of the woman who gave her life and taught her how to bake.

"Mom, what do you think of these? They're the first snow

skin mooncakes that I made on my own. Thank you for teaching me everything I needed to know." Tears came, and Cathy let them flow. "I'm in love, Mom. It's so scary in a good way. The Moon Goddess heard my prayer. I wanted to thank you for loving me and teaching me the meaning of love. I hope I've made you proud with these mooncakes. I added an extra pinch of salt just for you. I know you don't like them too sweet."

Satisfied after the much-needed chat with her mom, Cathy returned to the kitchen island and stared at the last two mooncakes saved for Daedriel. She dusted some powdered sugar in the shape of a heart on top of them. Then she placed them inside a box and tied it up. She'd give it to him tomorrow for their first August Moon tradition. The best magic was the kind you created yourself, and she was creating something extraordinary with her angel.

Her phone chimed with a text message from Daedriel. *Will be over at seven. Need to redeem my raincheck. Want some Lavandula wine?*

She grinned. *Yes, please. I hope you like Asian fusion food.*

I'll eat anything you make. For dessert, I'm going to eat you.

Cathy's heart jumped at his bluntness and the image that popped into her mind. Her thighs quivered as heat warmed her body. She didn't reply to his message. What could she say?

She pushed all sexual thoughts away to focus on the dinner entrée. If she kept standing there fantasizing about him, they'd both be starving tonight.

An hour later, she had a pan of longevity noodles with a dish of stir-fried kale, onions, snow peas, and garlic. She grilled some teriyaki-flavored chicken thighs with brown rice. Placing everything on a tray, she shoved it into the oven to keep warm.

As she removed her apron, doubts began to creep in. What if the food wasn't good enough for his otherworldly tastes? Well, she had frozen pizza in the freezer. That could work as an alternative option.

She sniffed herself. She smelled like garlic and chicken. Not the best scent for seduction. She had an exciting plan for him tonight. She'd be using her exercise equipment she hadn't practiced on in a while. What would he think of her?

Cathy glanced at the clock on the wall, which showed an hour before dinner time. After a quick shower, she stared at her closet, rummaging through her lingerie selection. She chose a soft blue set because of his blue eyes and wings. After she slipped on a blue maxi dress, she used a large-barrel curling iron to achieve big waves in her hair. She finished her look with some makeup that wasn't too dramatic.

She wanted him to remember this night in the same way she would remember the unforgettable journey along the East Coast, skimming the Atlantic Ocean and touching the mountaintops. Her dinner couldn't compare to what he'd given her, but her intention and heart were there.

Cathy's thoughts swung to her studio, an enormous project that he'd finished in no time at all. All that was left were minor things. In such a short amount of time, Cathy's life had transformed for the better because of this angel.

The doorbell rang, and she rushed down to greet him, almost forgetting her high heels.

TWENTY-ONE

Daedriel

When Cathy opened the door, Daedriel was starstruck. His quick reflexes prevented him from dropping the bottle of Lavandula wine. For a moment, he didn't breathe, enamored by her beauty and the cheerfulness in her brown eyes, which said she'd been waiting for him.

He loved knowing she'd been thinking about him. He hadn't been able to stop thinking about her. In the past, he'd laughed at friends who had fallen in love, doing silly things. He never understood it until now. Love was a powerful emotion that was difficult to explain. Perhaps that was its true power—to be mutable and mysterious.

Cathy wore a blue dress that hugged her fit body in a way that teased and taunted him, making him want to rip it off of her. Her hair had generous waves that mimicked those of the sea at night. She tucked it to the side with a sparkling clip. He'd never seen a more beautiful woman. His fingers itched to touch every inch of her. His member twitched in his leather pants as he perused her face and body. He wasn't sure if he'd be able to concentrate on dinner.

Daedriel reached for a lock of hair and twirled it around his finger. "You dressed up for me."

Cathy was a contrast to the darkness he'd just encountered in the nearby woods. He'd flown in search of the wave of dark energy. He thought it was Rask, but it turned out to be a gathering of blorvuses. He killed them with his seraph fire, but the dark energy from the soil continued to rise even as he tried to suffocate it. Whatever was happening underground was a force he hadn't come across. He had continued to search for Rask but came up with nothing. Daedriel prayed the Aurum Grid would provide helpful information. He could review the map with Eraton tomorrow.

"I did," Cathy said, emanating perfect contentment.

Daedriel wanted that smile splashed on her face constantly. There was too much darkness in the world, and he didn't want any of it to touch her.

He shoved all his concerns away to give her the full attention she deserved. Right now, no one else mattered but her.

Cathy eyed him from top to bottom, exciting every nerve-ending in his body. "You got dressed up too, Sexy Carpenter."

He snorted at the description. "Well, that's new."

"I love a man who's good with his hands." She tugged at the button-down shirt that wasn't completely buttoned and patted his leather pants. "I also love this business-casual dangerous look on you. Makes me wonder what kind of 'business' you're planning to negotiate tonight."

Business negotiations hadn't been on his mind, but he was an adaptable seraph. Very adaptable.

He smirked. "That depends on the offer, Hammer Goddess. Since we're going with nicknames today." He reached for the hammer tucked into the back of his waistband. "For you."

Cathy roared with laughter that echoed into the woods. "This is new for me too. Usually, men bring me flowers, not a hammer." But she held it tight to her chest like a bouquet. "I love it."

"It's yours." He wasn't sure if she would appreciate it. That hammer had been with him for hundreds of years. "But if you prefer flowers—"

"No. It's a novelty. It represents us—non-conventional. Look at us. We're standing in the doorway flirting. Who does that? Come inside so I can keep staring at you." She pulled him through the door and shut it behind her.

He placed the bottle of wine on the kitchen counter.

With a serious expression, she waved the hammer. "Are you sure about this? This is one of your magical tools. You used it to build my studio, and who knows what else in your lifetime."

"That's why I want to give it to you."

Her face softened as she examined the ancient symbols inscribed on the silver handle. "I don't even know how to use it."

"You will from this moment on." Daedriel wrapped his hands over hers while gripping the handle of the hammer. He whispered light language, which were ancient sounds the higher dimensions understood.

She is my love. She is my heart. Take care of her as you take care of me.

Cathy gasped as heat and light radiated from the handle and traveled to the hammer's head, claw, and face. As it vibrated, Daedriel released his grip, allowing Cathy to hold the handle. The hammer increased in size, the head changing into various shapes for her review. Still glowing, the hammer replicated itself before coming back to the master one in her hand.

In awe, she glanced at him and smiled. "It's not heavy like I thought it would be."

"That's because it's making itself lightweight for you."

Cathy closed her eyes like she was communicating with it. When she opened them, the hammer stopped glowing and returned to its normal size. "I told it to stop glowing, and it works! It understands me!"

He'd give a thousand years of his life for that joy to stay on her face.

She put the hammer down on the kitchen counter and threw her arms around him. "Thank you for this magical gift."

He planned on giving her all the most magical things life could offer.

Cathy's hands lowered to his ass and squeezed. "I've wanted to do that for a long time."

Daedriel lowered his hands and claimed what belonged to him. "Great minds think alike." Sexual energy roared in him. "Dinner can wait. I want dessert first."

She smirked. "Okay, Sexy Carpenter. I've got a pole for you to inspect. Let me know if it measures up to your standards."

TWENTY-TWO

Cathy

"A pole?" Daedriel arched a dark eyebrow. "I'm intrigued."

With a change in plans, Cathy placed a gentle hand on his chest. His heart pounded against her palm. "Give me five minutes, and then you can come upstairs. First room on the right."

He flared his nostrils. "That's torture."

"Trust me, you'll enjoy it. It's an artistic way of introducing you to my body. You'll get to see me in the air. I've never done this for anyone before." She pecked him on the lips, teasing.

His blue eyes flashed with need. "Five minutes. That's it."

Smiling, Cathy rushed up to her bedroom, took out her stainless-steel dancing pole, and set it up. It didn't take long to secure the base of the pole to the floor and ceiling mounts. Anticipation rushed through her as she stripped off her maxi dress. The evening had escalated to spontaneity. She had planned on having dinner, chatting for a bit, and then she'd introduce him to her bedroom. But now, she was going with the flow.

She stood next to her pole wearing a blue bra and matching underwear. Her cheeks burned at what she was about to do. She hadn't known how much core workout and strength training were required for pole dancing until she took classes. It had started as a dare from her friends, but she fell in love with it. It was fun and different from going to the gym. She'd firmed up her abs, thighs, and legs from all the various poses, which she hadn't shown to anyone. Tonight, her seraph would be the first person to see this side of her.

"Damaat." Daedriel's sexy voice sent a chill down her spine.

Cathy turned, met his gaze, and her skin tingled as though he was breathing on it. He stepped into the room, his eyes scanning her body.

"I hope you'll enjoy this artistic performance."

"I'm already enjoying it. You know how to arouse me." He walked up closer, his blue eyes flaring like liquid fire.

Cathy's heart raced from the intensity of his gaze. She leaned back against the pole, and the metal surface cooled her warm body. She arched, flicked him a seductive look, and began her performance. She jumped and grabbed the pole, pulling herself up. She performed the martini spin and paused at the pole sit.

"Don't move." He walked up to her and supported her butt with one hand. He walked his fingers up her spine, over her shoulder to land on her breast. "I'm jealous of this pole. It got to touch you before I did. I might have to destroy it."

Cathy let out a quiet laugh. "I'm not attracted to the pole. I have several of them, actually."

"There's one seraph 'pole' aching for you, Hammer Goddess." He palmed his bulge.

She smirked as heat pooled at her core, wanting him, desperately wanting *that* pole.

Daedriel's hand adored one breast, then the other. "I love that you planned this event for me. I'm going to personalize it. You're mine, Cathy." With a flick of his finger, her bra and underwear flew off her body and landed on the other side of the room, leaving her completely bare to him.

She gasped as excitement skated down her spine. He brushed his hand against her nipples and lowered his mouth to claim one.

Cathy moaned and arched into his mouth. If it weren't for his hand supporting her suspension, she'd probably fall. She hadn't expected him to love her while she was on the pole. But the newness of it thrilled her.

"Show me your moves, Cathy." Daedriel stepped back, and six iridescent blue wings flung out from behind him. The feathers glistened and glowed as though he was the moon in her bedroom. His white shirt and black leather pants joined her bra and underwear on the other side of the room.

Cathy slowed her breath as she took in his naked bronzed body corded with muscles. She stared at the glorious length of him, and it twitched. He was more than a man—and he was hers.

In this moment, they were bare to each other in heart and soul. Nothing stood between them. No darkness, no doubts, no immortality versus mortality, nothing but the passion in the room.

Love and courage surged in Cathy as she twisted herself into the bird of paradise position, where her head faced the ground, her legs in a wide split like a professional gymnast. She was now exposed to him in ways that should embarrass her. She had no panties covering her most private part.

Daedriel growled and approached her. "Damaat, Cathy."

A soft wing supported her, another cupping her body. Her arms relaxed with the support.

Her stomach flipped with excitement when his fingers danced along her inner thighs, heading toward her core. "You are so beautiful."

Her thighs quivered when he replaced his fingers with his mouth. She gasped when his lips pressed to her center. With both hands, he held up her butt, keeping her legs apart, and devoured. Sensation shot through her body, sending out waves and waves of pleasure that brought her to life. She closed her eyes and dove into the sea of bliss spreading from her core to every corner of her body.

She'd never been loved like this. She sensed a spinning motion and opened her eyes. Daedriel had lifted her away from the pole, winged himself over to her bed, and dropped her onto the mattress.

His wings cocooned them. "I want you comfortable when I take you."

She dragged his mouth to hers as need assailed her. He kissed her with primordial hunger, sending fire zipping through her veins. His tongue tangled with hers, and she loved the citrus flavor that was uniquely him. He tasted like ancient wine only improved with time. When his mouth left hers to nuzzle at her neck, she turned, giving him all the access he wanted. His masculine and musky scent made her want to bite him. She pressed her face into his neck and nipped at the vein pulsing for her.

He growled, allowing her to bite and suckle his skin. She'd never wanted anyone the way she wanted him. With him, she felt safe and whole again.

His face and body misted with sweat as he lowered himself. The stalk of heat pulsed between her thighs. He met her gaze, and passion radiated from the blue eyes that glowed like his wings. The irises shifted as if water currents flowed in them. She would never forget how she looked in them—a woman in love.

She lifted a hand to his face as heat spiraled inside her. She opened her thighs wider for him. "Take me."

TWENTY-THREE

Daedriel

Love surged in him as he waved a hand, conjuring a condom over his length.

"There are definitely magical perks to making love with an angel," she whispered.

"I have plenty of tricks to show you, love." He positioned himself at her center and teased her.

Pulsing with desire, Daedriel slid inside her, loving how her eyes darkened for him.

She moaned as her muscles tightened around him. "I bet you've never had a pole dancer like me." She lifted her hips, taking him in deeper, torturing and tantalizing him all at once.

"I don't want anyone playing with my pole but you." Emotions swelled in him as she laughed.

Her nails dug into his back and raked a lovely line down his spine that opened his soul. His body released the loneliness that had gripped him all these years. That release made more room for him to love.

He kissed her, wanting to claim every part of her. He inhaled a hypnotizing hint of lavender and savored the taste of something sweet and delectable. He broke the kiss to look at her as though he wanted her face imprinted in his vision forever—imprinted on his soul. She looked sated and seductive. A bead of sweat from him dripped onto her forehead, and he kissed it away. Her delicate skin slicked under his touch.

She smiled, and the gentle way she brushed his face made him surrender. Daedriel from the Seraphim Angel Order yielded to this woman he loved. The diamond crystal in his heart shone even brighter.

Her body tensed, and he drove deeper into her. She let out a cry as tension coiled in him. "Come with me."

His name escaped her mouth, and his heart leaped as her body shuddered against his. Pleasure ricocheted down his spine, and he roared, "Cathy!"

He kissed her forehead again, took a few seconds to catch his breath, and rolled onto his side. She grabbed his hand and clutched it to her heart. "Was that divine intervention? Or divine intention?"

"Divine affirmation." He grinned, admiring her beautiful and sarcastic mind. He shifted to his side, looking at her. The diamond light emanating from his heart turned his skin translucent.

"Oh my gosh! What is that?" Cathy bolted up in bed. "What's happened to your chest?"

Daedriel sat up, rearranged the pillow behind his head. "The seraphim angels have a diamond-shaped crystal inside their hearts. It's something we all have, but it's dormant until activated. Most angels live without it ever being activated. I haven't heard of many with the diamond heart activation. You gave me this gift, Cathy. The diamond light activates from the purest love given and received. You unlocked my heart."

Cathy's eyes glistened as she traced her fingers around the diamond outline. "What do you mean by 'love given?'"

Daedriel cupped her chin. "It means I *love* you. I know it's probably too soon to say those words. I wasn't planning on telling you until later. I wanted to give you time to adjust to our relationship, time for you to know that when I speak those words, I truly mean them. I didn't want you to think I was sweet-talking you."

Streams of tears rolled down her cheek. He grabbed a tissue from the box on the nightstand and offered it to her. Though joy splashed on her face, there was doubt in her eyes. He knew the sensitive topic of her mortality and his immortality concerned her. That was something they would discuss another day. He didn't want to ruin this perfect night by bringing up a subject that worried him too. How could he be with her forever if she couldn't live forever like him?

Daedriel shoved that anxiety away and pulled her into an embrace with her head on his shoulders. He listened to her heartbeat while her hand covered his diamond heart. There would be no one else for him. He would find a way to give her that forever.

Tomorrow, he'd find Rask and eliminate the darkness surrounding Cathy. Then he'd think about how he could remain with her while still serving the SAO.

"I love you too." She whispered as she drifted off to sleep.

Her words sent a jolt to his diamond heart. New energy electrified him, rushing up and down his body and skipping along his skin like sparks of celebration. It fired up the nerves in his brain, giving him the answer he needed.

With a smile on his face and hope in his heart, he joined her in sleep.

TWENTY-FOUR

Daedriel

Eraton arrived at ten in the morning and splashed a copy of the Aurum Grid in the air in Daedriel's office. The suspended map depicted an energetic grid surrounding the Earth like a gold net.

Crossing his arms, Daedriel studied the ley lines running around Earth. He stared at the thicker lines, which created the macrosystem of the grid. The smaller ley lines created the microsystem. He considered this Aurum Grid like the bodily systems where the thicker ley lines were the arteries and veins and the capillaries were the smaller meridians. No matter the size, they all played an important role in the health of the Earth and the Universe.

In the same way disease could infect blood vessels, dark energy could infect the grid. Daedriel would do everything he could to stop this disease from spreading.

Uncrossing his arms, Daedriel pointed to the dark spot pulsing from New Hampshire in the United States of America.

"This is where the infection started. It's the burst of darkness from the Reversal Black Tourmaline."

Eraton nodded. "Rask brought the stone here because dark energy had already taken root here. The bastard just gave it a boost."

"Today's full moon will amplify both dark and light energy. Rask will surely take advantage of it," Daedriel said as a spot of darkness vibrated from the energetic map. "Something's happening here." He zoomed into the Aurum Grid. "That's not too far from this location. Ready to hunt?"

An orange flame flickered in Eraton's eyes. "Let's go get them."

Blue and orange wings flew to a secluded cabin about twenty miles away. Darkness dominated the area covered with trees. He cut through the web of density that kept the cabin secluded, and descended. When his feet touched the ground, the heaviness weighed like chains trying to imprison him to this place that was steeped with menace. The air produced an uncomfortable bite. In addition, there was something else in the atmosphere that made his eyes droopy.

Daedriel inhaled a deep breath, connecting to the power within him to keep him awake. He turned to Eraton. "Don't fall asleep on me."

"You're not my type," Eraton retorted sarcastically. "What kind of shit is this? It wants to strip our consciousness."

"Some kind of mind control manipulation." Daedriel had scoured this area before, but why hadn't he noticed the darkness then?

Movement in the area appeared slow. A leaf fell from a nearby tree and took a while to reach the ground. The soil and the trees lacked essence. Whatever was here had stripped the life from them. Though the ground and trees appeared normal, Daedriel didn't sense strong life force pulsing from them. The scenery could have been a façade to steer intruders away.

Daedriel folded back the set of wings. He kept the other wings hidden.

Eraton also hid his four wings, folding one back, gesturing to his ears. Noises erupted like a murder of crows. Hundreds of the two-headed blorvuses flew out from the cabin windows. Daedriel drew out his flaming sword and slashed at the evil birds.

With his orange-flamed sword, Eraton killed the swarm of attacking blorvuses preventing him from entering the cabin. Daedriel tapped into the seraph fire behind his eyes and seared the remaining blorvuses. They thudded to the ground in piles.

"You go check it out. I'll clean this up and join you." Eraton's eyes glowed orange as he singed the dead blorvuses into ashes.

Cautiously, Daedriel entered the cabin, expecting to find Rask. Dark clouds filled the cabin, and eerie voices came from a wall with a dark tunnel spinning at the center. Daedriel couldn't make out what the voices were saying.

The wind picked up in the cabin, pushing him toward the tunnel. The metallic smell of blood and death burned his nose. The voices grew louder.

"Join us, Daedriel from the Seraphim Angel Order." The grinding sound with the howling wind made it difficult for him to hone in on the voice. Who was it? Did he know this being? Or was it a spirit that Rask created?

Large critters with red eyes ran across the walls. The cabin reeked of death and decay.

Where was Rask? Daedriel gripped his sword and shot a blue flame into the spinning tunnel. Screams echoed as the tunnel dismantled and the dark clouds faded. His eyes sent a powerful blaze of seraph fire into the crumbling tunnel. Fire hissed as it met an energy. An eruption burst somewhere inside the tunnel, and then embers filled the cabin.

Eraton entered and waved the floating embers away from his face, covering his nose. "What the hell was in here?"

"Rask is pulling in darkness from the DAA and planting it in here, at this location. Let's burn this place down." As he headed back out the door, a photograph floated across his vision.

Daedriel caught it in his hand, and his heart stopped as he stared at Cathy's picture.

TWENTY-FIVE

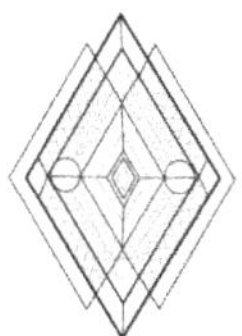

Cathy

She spent a few hours moving some books from her upstairs office to the new studio. Cathy also brought her office chair out of storage. She would take her time with the interior decoration.

She smiled as thoughts from last night surfaced in her mind. She couldn't believe he made love to her while she was clinging to the pole. It was sexy, like something out of this world. She had a naked angel with gorgeous blue wings devouring her in the most intimate place. She wanted more of that excitement.

Her body shivered from the memory. The former office would now be her pole dancing and exercise room. She and Daedriel could discuss other ideas to make the room more innovative.

Now that those tasks were all set, her mind concentrated on the August Moon celebration for tonight. She took out the box with snow skin mooncakes and placed them on the counter. She'd give them to Daedriel after making her wish to the Moon Goddess.

She patted the pile of greeting cards, all written and drawn with his feather. She couldn't wait to show him. He had inspired her new greeting card collection. She'd been having a tough time thinking of a new collection, but thankfully an angel entered and illuminated an idea.

She'd drawn a few samples that came out perfect. They were simple line abstractions with a dash of watercolor to give it a soft and ethereal effect. The collection would be called "The Divine Intention Series." Her marketing team at Luminous Press would have fun promoting that.

As she held the hammer Daedriel had given her, she recalled how he had told her he loved her. She felt the truth in his words and from the vibration of his diamond heart. She had also said those words to him. Love was a strange emotion. It came like a storm and took her on an unforgettable flight, one that continued to astound her.

Not only did he construct her studio—something that meant the world to her and her mom—he also reconstructed her life and her belief in love. Daedriel gave her hope again. He made her believe in true love. In some strange way, he was the moon that illuminated her life. Because of him, she felt complete.

She held the hammer close to her heart, and the handle glowed as if it felt her emotion. Where could she put this hammer? It needed its own place. She didn't want it in her tool belt. This magical gift was more than just a hammer.

For now, she placed it on the bottom of her kitchen counter. She went to heat the longevity noodles she'd made yesterday. Daedriel had a little of it before he left this morning for some meeting. She had given him the bag of nuts and fresh vegetables she'd bought for Tika and invited the parrot over tonight for some mooncakes.

A sudden chill skittered down her spine, and the hair on her neck erected, catching her attention. Fearing a blorvus was nearby, she looked out the window but didn't see anything.

She jumped when Victor knocked on her door. She forgot about the uncomfortable feeling and opened the door for him.

"Great timing, Victor. I made some mooncakes for you and Rosa. I gave you four. You can give some to Lizzi." She walked over to the counter and grabbed the box for him.

The cold chill returned, and for some reason, the outdoors looked gloomy, though there had been evening light minutes ago.

Why was Victor so quiet? Did something happen to Rosa?

Cathy whirled around to ask him, and her stomach twisted in terror. Victor's eyes rolled back as black mist oozed from his neck, shoulders, and chest like vapory serpents. Freed from its confines, the dark vapor increased in density, forming arms, legs, and a head with an appalling face. When the dark spirit completely detached from Victor, he collapsed to the ground.

Heart thumping, Cathy's mind raced for a way to get to Victor, but terror glued her feet to the ground as the electricity in her house flashed on and off. The air thickened, making it difficult for her to breathe. Was Victor okay? She remembered Daedriel mentioning about the darkness taking over a host body, especially someone going through difficulties.

The wispy spirit expanded in size and morphed into a demon with bat wings. Fear stabbed at her. Was this the enemy Daedriel had been searching for? Was it here for him? Love for him billowed in her, pushing the terror aside.

She dug for courage, trying to sound calm. "Are you Rask?"

"I am. And you're the love that has changed Daedriel." His voice had a strange echo.

She swallowed. "What do you want? Daedriel isn't here."

Rask's lips curled. "I'm not here for him." A serpent of dark energy wrapped around her hands. "You'll be the sacrifice for the Dark Angel Agenda."

Rask dragged her out of her kitchen, the serpent rope tied around her wrists. As they entered the woods, Cathy tugged against her binds, not wanting to go with him, but the dark ties tightened and hissed. Pain burst in her wrists. "Keep fighting, and the ties will burn your hands off."

Though fear gripped her, she screamed, praying someone would hear her. "Help me! Someone, please help me!"

A layer of darkness rose from the soil in her backyard. A rancid stench churned her stomach. The darkness turned the grass and the trees black.

"I offer you a seraph's lover. Her blood will empower the DAA's mission."

"Did you invite him to join our legion?" This evil voice came from the layer of darkness that elevated from the ground. The vibration from the voice chilled her bones.

"I did, but he refused. Please let Master know I tried my best." Rask spoke to the layer of darkness that formed into several monstrous faces and stopped when it became a huge serpent. Smaller serpents sprouted from its body like a terrifying Gorgon.

A grunt erupted from the enormous snake with three red eyes. A small snake stretched out to snap at her, and Cathy ran with her wrists still tied. She didn't get far as something wrapped around her waist, pulling her toward the giant serpent.

"No! Let me go!"

Where was Daedriel? Did Rask do something to him already? Her chest ached, fearing she'd never see him again.

A familiar warmth brushed her cheek, and she glanced up toward the sky and saw the full moon with the gold rim around it. The gold rim disappeared in seconds, but she understood its message to her. The moon illuminated the danger, giving her a way out. The glint of the moon reminded her of her hammer.

She remembered how she'd given it directions. Cathy closed her eyes and called to the hammer. *Help me! Kill these demons!*

In an instant, she heard glass shatter as a glowing hammer spiraled toward her. The claw of the hammer gleamed like blades as it severed the snake around her waist. Wails and shrieks exploded in the woods as more snakes slithered and flung themselves at her.

Multiply.

Twenty gleaming hammers appeared before her, smashing and slicing the evil snakes. The large serpent curled its head like a cobra watching. The slits of three eyes widened as if in fury. While she pounded at a snake near her feet with a hammer, Rask flung a force at her that knocked her to the ground. The hammer fell from her grip, and Rask threw a web of energy over it. Because the master hammer was now restrained, the replicas were weakened too. They faded in and out, struggling to remain present.

Cathy had to do something. With her hands to the ground, she grabbed a fistful of soil.

When Rask approached her, she whipped the soil into his face. She pushed herself up and ran.

A flash of white wings came to her aid. "Run, Cathy!"

Tika beat his wings, sending a cloud of white dust to block Rask. But the demon pitched out a dark force that threw the bird against the tree. A painful sound escaped the parrot.

"Tika!" Cathy shouted and ran toward her friend, but Rask gripped her by the throat as sharp nails dug into her skin.

TWENTY-SIX

Daedriel

He felt her fear. He felt her pain.

Moon energy dominated the woods, and he knew Cathy had connected to it somehow. A gold rim glowed around the moon. As he descended, it blessed him with a potent force that electrified his diamond heart.

Fury spiked in Daedriel when he spotted Rask's hand over Cathy's throat. Daedriel's blood roared as seraph fire shot out from his eyes, slamming into Rask's back. With the activation of his diamond heart and now with the moon's blessings, Daedriel's power had multiplied tremendously. The wide gash on Rask's back proved the extent of Daedriel's power.

"I'll deal with them." Eraton flew toward the serpents with his orange blade in hand.

Daedriel landed beside Cathy and ran a hand over the red marks on her throat. He'd desecrate Rask for putting his hands on her.

"Are you okay?" Daedriel asked.

"I'm fine, but Tika's hurt." She gestured to his injured parrot.

"Go take him to safety."

Cathy hesitated. "Are you sure? Will you be okay?"

Even when terror filled every fiber of her being, she worried about him.

"I'm fine. Go." He released the net around his hammer and sent it to accompany Cathy and Tika.

Daedriel walked over to Rask, standing over his quaking body. Blood pooled around him as dark vapors surfaced from his body. Daedriel sent a blast of blue flames into the dark vapors, devouring them. The flames hissed as they devoured the defiant darkness.

A beam of moonlight pierced through the trees and illuminated a portion of Rask's body. Half of him was in shadows, the other was lit. Was this a sign for Daedriel to consider when he killed Rask? That his former friend still had some light in him?

Rask looked up at Daedriel and struggled to open his mouth to speak. His features had changed from their last encounter. The demonic eyes had disappeared, and for a moment, Daedriel recognized his former friend.

"I'm... sorry." The words choked out of Rask as blood filled his mouth. "I... didn't mean for this to happen. The darkness manipulated me, consumed me. I envied the seraphim brotherhood. I only wanted power to be like you. The DAA promised me power if I gave them the Reversal Black Tourmaline. But something happened to me, and I don't remember why I'm here. I don't even recognize myself."

Rask winced in pain as more blood bled from him and black vapors flowed from the wounds.

As Daedriel's blue flame ingested more dark vapors, he understood Rask had been possessed. Negative emotions allowed for a negative walk-in to take over the body, mind, and soul. That was how the dark played this game of manipulation.

Was Daedriel still angry at his former friend? Yes. But did Rask deserve an excruciating death? No.

"Daedriel, you must be careful. The DAA has a bigger plan for Earth. This is the birthing ground for demons... the Reversal Black Tourmaline only fertilized it..." Rask winced, struck silent by the pain.

Daedriel met Rask's eyes, and his former friend understood his intention.

"Do it. End my pain... I deserve it."

Daedriel's eyes speared seraph fire into Rask's heart and then his head, wiping out areas where life could thrive.

After he burned Rask's body and cleaned the area, he helped Eraton do the same to the snakes. They cleared the soil and the woods of dark energy as best they could.

For now, the immediate threat was over. When would the Dark Angel Agenda strike again? It was hard to tell, and no one could predict that.

But Daedriel and his brothers would be ready.

He glanced up at the full moon and gave it a nod of respect. He appreciated its blessings and the wisdom it offered him. The full moon represented the full cycle of his mission and illuminated the completion of his soul.

Daedriel couldn't wait to start a new phase of his life with Cathy.

TWENTY-SEVEN

Cathy

Two days after the horrific ordeal, Cathy and Daedriel finally had a chance to enjoy a belated August Moon celebration.

Daedriel had conjured up a stone table and bench down by the lake where the peaceful evening sky hung low in hues of purple and blue. The atmosphere showed no indication of what had transpired days ago.

Cathy made new longevity noodles for lunch, and he brought a bottle of Lavandula wine. It was a simple dinner just for the two of them.

"How's Tika? Where's your brother Eraton? He's very nice and good-looking too."

Daedriel flicked her a glance.

She smiled. "I guess all seraphim angels are good-looking, but the most stunning of them all is you. *My* angel."

A cocky smile curved on his lips. "Tika is doing fine. He's visiting friends and will return with Eraton and some other members of the SAO in a few days."

"More angels are coming? How long will they be staying?" she asked.

"They'll stay at my place for a while. The house is furnished now. It's large enough to house all of them. I have plenty of room. My brothers and I will continue to monitor this area until the Aurum Grid shows that all the darkness has been removed."

She couldn't help her inquiry. "Is Earth's moon dying because of the darkness presently here?"

"No. There's an ethereal force monitoring Earth's moon. Furthermore, your moon was intentionally placed in Earth's orbit, remember? So the energetic link is different from those moons that naturally come with its planet. Regardless, your moon has developed its own consciousness over time, and the frequency tells me that it's also fighting the dark from within."

Cathy recalled how the gold rim around the moon had brought her awareness back to the hammer during that critical moment. In fact, the moon had watched her growth all these years. And she couldn't help believing that there was a goddess or some sacred being up there. Whatever it was, she was grateful for its presence, guidance, and light all these years.

"I think the ethereal force around the moon has a gold rim," she said.

Smiling, he nodded. "I saw it too. I think the moon approves of our relationship."

She looked up at the waning moon with its light decreasing from fullness. "I love that idea."

Her mind returned to the Aurum Grid and the ley lines that surrounded Earth. Daedriel had shown her the energy grid earlier today. Though they removed one pocket of darkness, there were still others brewing.

"I noticed one ley line was brightly lit. What does that mean?"

"I was told that when the diamond heart is activated by love, it unlocks a rare celestial energy that's been woven into the grid."

Her eyes beamed. "Really? You mean, we unlocked a new ley line? We unlocked a new divine force?" She learned something new each day with him.

Daedriel clasped her hand. "We did. You unlocked me too. I was trapped in my own world until you came along. You offered me love, and that opened my heart and solidified my purpose even more. Before you, I fought for my realm. Now, I'm fighting for you. For *us*. Because without you, there is no light in me." He lifted her hand for a kiss.

Her heart swelled with love. "I guess I did unlock the angel." She drew his hand to her heart. "And now I want to give him a key to my house and ask him to move in with me. Will you?" Her eyes fluttered, and he laughed. "I have a room with a *special* pole that needs some creative ideas."

His eyes narrowed. "Since I'll be spending all my time with you, it makes the most sense. I've got *special* ideas for this room."

She got up from her seat, sat on his lap, and threw her arms around him. "What about your sanctuary? Will you miss visiting it? I'll miss it..." She wanted to return to that magical place again with all the mountains and moons. The lifeless moon still gripped her heart.

"My sanctuary is multidimensional. It goes where I take it. So I can move it to the room with the *special* pole." He grinned and rubbed his thumb over a scratch on her hand.

Despite the terrors she witnessed, Cathy came away with only a few scratches. She didn't want to go to the hospital and have the doctors and nurses ask questions she couldn't answer. How would she explain everything? She didn't want the news reporters stationed outside her home, waiting to see angels and demons. Would they believe her if she told them the truth?

They'd just think she was crazy. Besides, she had a business to protect; she didn't need that kind of attention.

So she had let Daedriel treat her at home. His celestial balm was better than any standard antibiotic.

Victor also believed in the supernatural and didn't say a word to the hospital staff. The hospital discovered he had a weak heart, and the stress from Rosa's illness made it worse.

"How's Victor?" Daedriel asked, nuzzling the crevice of her neck.

"He's fine. He's cutting back on work to take care of Rosa. Rosa's healing beautifully, according to their daughter, Lizzi. She's moving back here to help sell her parent's business. But Victor and Rosa still want to help me. I'll be their *only* customer. At least I don't need to search for a new cleaning service."

"Works out well for you."

Cathy got off his lap and retrieved the box of mooncakes from her bag. "I have a gift for you. I made these to celebrate the August Moon with you, but life happened." She placed it in front of him and took out a blue paper plate. "It's still fresh. They're good for at least a week."

He opened them and stared. "You made these? They look like little moons." He held one in his hand.

"Mooncakes symbolize completeness, sweetness, unity, family, love, and dreams come true. I want all of those things for you and more. Remember the legend I told you about the Moon Goddess? That you can ask her for anything during this celebration?"

He nodded as he placed the mooncakes on the plate.

Her heart hammered as she confessed. "Each of these mooncakes is baked with a wish I made for you."

His blue eyes liquefied. "What did you wish for me?"

"For the revival of the Oriss moon in your sanctuary. When I was there, I didn't feel like it was completely lifeless. I think it still has hope. It matters to you, so it matters to me." She inhaled a deep breath before continuing. "After you showed me that 'movie' of your life filled with blood and death, it bothered me that you didn't have enough love around. So I asked the Moon Goddess to gift that to you."

Daedriel cupped her face with both hands and kissed her. The heat of the diamond heart radiated through her.

"You're the moon to my life, Cathy. To me, you're the magic and light. You've given me so much. It's all priceless. I have love, peace, and hope because of you. Thank you. As for the Oriss, we'll have to make a visit and see what happens."

She couldn't wait to revisit his sanctuary.

His eyes bore into hers. "I have a couple of things to give you too."

TWENTY-EIGHT

Daedriel

He waved a hand, and a pile of paper boats sat on the table.

Cathy gasped. "Oh my goodness, I totally forgot about them. When did you retrieve them?"

"I came back to check out the area the day after you released them and noticed you'd forgotten to fetch them from your little lagoon. I didn't want the wind blowing them somewhere else. They were your prayers, so I saved them for you."

"Thank you. I sent out some well-wishes for everyone with these boats. Sometimes, it's good to send a prayer for joy and peace to everyone and let the Universe deliver how it sees fit. I did say a prayer for myself on one of those boats."

He lifted an eyebrow. "What did you pray for?"

"For clarity." She looked at him. "When I first met you, I felt something between us. Something powerful and inexplicable. I was afraid of my own emotions. What if they were illusions? So I asked for clarity, and I got my answer. My feelings are true and real."

"My feelings are true and real too," he said. "I love that you're generous with everyone. You give a lot to others." He tapped his chest where his diamond heart glowed. "I know you love me, and I love you. But I also know you're concerned about your mortality versus my immortality."

"I... I can't stop thinking that I will die one day and leave you all alone again." Tears filled her eyes. It seemed like she'd been crying a lot ever since she met him. But they were joyful tears.

"I know." Daedriel took her hand and placed it over his heart. "But you don't have to worry about it anymore."

"Why not?"

"As part of my diamond heart activation, I can offer immortality to one soul. I confirmed this with the Elders from my realm. It's true, and I'm gifting it to you. Would you like to be with me forever?"

Her mouth dropped open as happiness gleamed in her eyes. "You're my only family left. If I could live forever, it would only be with you." A slight hesitation flashed in her eyes. "Does it hurt to change? I mean the transformation process."

He smiled. "No. Your connection to the moon will help you transition even better. Moon frequency adds a gentleness to everything. Also, I'll be assisting you. It won't happen overnight. It will take a while for your body and mind to acclimate. There are a few steps, and one of them requires you to eat plasma fruits. They are delicious."

Daedriel hadn't expected to find love when he came to Earth, but now that he found it, he'd protect it with his life. He found a partner who loved him, an eternal purpose that empowered him. Because of her, he became a stronger seraph, a stronger warrior to defend the Celestial Realm and what he believed in. He believed that love had the power to change and heal. He couldn't wait to help Cathy transition into her immortality.

He rose from his chair and offered her a hand. "Would you like to visit my sanctuary and start the immortality process now? Or you can wait. My offer doesn't expire. We have all the time in the world."

She twisted her lips in a way that made him want to kiss her. She tossed him a mischievous look. "It can wait till tomorrow. For today, I think we should experiment on the dancing pole."

He grinned and scooped her into his arm. "I think that should be our daily routine."

"Sounds like a plan. Why don't you show me all your skills, Mr. Sexy Carpenter?"

With a heart full of love and diamond light, Daedriel showed Cathy how much he loved her.

Thank you so much for reading! I hope you enjoyed Cathy and Daedriel's story. Read Lizzi and Eraton's story in **Unchain the Angel**. Coming soon! Don't miss out on any new releases. Sign up for my newsletter!

http://callazae.com/newsletter/

If you enjoyed this story, I'd love it if you'd consider leaving me a review on your favorite retailer website.

I invite you to join my Facebook reader's group, where I offer sneak peeks, giveaways, special perks, and other book news! **https://www.facebook.com/groups/callazae**

Soldiers of Saedo Collection 1: Books 1 - 4

You can now get books 1-4 in one collection!

https://callazae.com/books/

AUDIOBOOKS are available for my Soldiers of Saedo Series!

An Alien Rescue (Soldiers of Saedo, #1)

An Alien Crush (Soldiers of Saedo, #2)

An Alien Dare (Soldiers of Saedo, #3)

An Alien Storm (Soldiers of Saedo, #4)

An Alien Lore (Soldiers of Saedo, #5)-Soon!

An Alien Spark (Soldiers of Saedo, #6)-Soon!

An Alien Future (Soldiers of Saedo, #7)-Soon!

(Soldiers of Saedo, #1)

"You weren't the only one who was rescued. We saved each other."

Emma is on vacation with her six siblings to ring in the New Year with everything auspicious and nothing to do with broken relationships, disappointments, and heartache. But what she got was an alien abduction.

Raeko, a beautiful green star-being, rescues her from horrific beasts that want her to reproduce for them. His protection and honesty stirs her heart in a way that echoes the love she has always wanted.

Is he Emma's New Year's gift? Or is he another male who's going to bruise her heart?

www.callazae.com/books

(Soldiers of Saedo, #2)

"A promise is sacred to me, and I had to fulfill it so I could woo you appropriately."

When a heroic star-being saves Sasha from horrific beasts, she develops a crush on him, sparking hope in her heart. But then he disappears. Taking matters into her own hands, Sasha tracks him down.

Maeson, a remarkable soldier who values his word, is attracted to Sasha, but a promise keeps him from her. In order to return to her, he must first fulfill his obligation to someone else and stop a dire threat from destroying them both.

Can Maeson offer Sasha what she needs? Or will he crush her heart?

www.callazae.com/books

(Soldiers of Saedo, #3)

"I love challenges, and you're the most captivating challenge to cross my path. I will unravel you."

Though excited to showcase her first galactic fashion show, Inga is stressed because she's desperate for one more model. A stunning star-being with the perfect body emerges, but his ego irritates her. Annoyed, she dares him to model for her, not expecting a challenge to her heart.

Osayik, an outstanding soldier with no interest in "strutting" down some runway—whatever that means—can't resist a challenge. Fascinated by Inga, he wants to know what lies beneath the beauty.

Does he dare listen to his heart? Or will pride get in his way?

www.callazae.com/books

(Soldiers of Saedo, #4)

"There's something different about you… Something untamed. Something mysterious. It's driving me crazy."

Battered and bruised from a previous relationship, Vanessa now prefers a quiet life as a chef on a new planet. But then a captivating star-being storms into her life and whips up a whirlwind of emotions that makes her heart yearn for things she has long forgotten.

Arkon, a skilled soldier who prefers numbers, charts, and anything with absoluteness is attracted to Vanessa. But she favors no rules and lures him out of his comfort zone. Having been scorned once, he fears she will burn him.

Is their union a recipe for love or destruction?

www.callazae.com/books

"She arrived on this new planet with two hot suns, but it was this blue warrior who burned away all her doubts."

As Captain of the Norakian warriors, Kazstrom anticipates the upcoming competition that can promote him to be the next General of his legion. But a poisonous wound threatens to eliminate his dream. The hunt for a cure leads him to Earth, where he encounters an alluring human female who not only possesses the moonstone he desperately needs, but she also ignites something deep within him. Intrigued, he is compelled to protect her from enemies who are after the same moonstone.

Teegan, a second-grade teacher, is drowning in debt and doubt after a failed engagement when a stunning star-being asks her to go to his planet and heal him. With nothing to lose, she decides a mini out-of-this-world adventure with Kazstrom is the exact escape required to alleviate her life's issues. But her heart has its own plans and tosses her into an escalating romance filled with danger that will leave them both shattered if they are not careful.

As Kazstrom battles his worst enemy to protect his starmate, Teegan must find her warrior spirit to defend the star-being she has come to love.

www.callazae.com/books

"Love is the most powerful frequency in all dimensions. It creates many realities that can save us. Or destroy us."

Orphaned as a child, Aleeya is now a warrior with standards and expectations. The search for her past leads her to defy a powerful darkness that could annihilate everyone she cares about. An attractive human shows her that her defiance is the key that battles the darkness and unlocks her heart.

Kenzo, a bounty hunter living in the shadows, encounters a stunning star-being who tempts his heart. But the thirst for vengeance for his brothers' killer prevents him from love. Can he defy his own demons to find salvation in her?

As the false light grows, Aleeya and Kenzo must join forces to fight for love and truth before darkness reigns supreme.

For a complete list of my books:

www.callazae.com/books

AUTHOR'S NOTE - NEW SERIES

Dear Readers,

I'm excited to share that I'll be releasing a contemporary romance series very soon. I love writing romance whether it's set in a fantastical world or the current world we live in. Love is magical no matter where it exists. I hope you'll enjoy these new stories.

If you're reading this message, that means you've read most of my books. (Thank you so much!) So you already know my writing style. You can expect the same in this new series. I've created two logos to differentiate my otherworldly stories to my contemporary stories. Hopefully, they'll give you an idea of what to expect for all of my books.

Once again, thank you for reading my work and inspiring me to continue writing.

Here is the prequel to my Etched series, Etched in the Arrangement. This is a novella that will give you a glimpse into the characters and setting around Boston and its surrounding towns. All other books after the prequel will be full-length novels.

Gemma

As a florist, my experience with cheating men makes me see them as rotten plants that can't be saved; they ruin the beauty of bouquets. I'm careful who I let into my life. Gorgeous things often have unseen thorns, so when an attractive man asks me out, I said no. But I have a problem: I can't stop thinking about him.

Tyson

I wear confidence and charm like an irresistible six-pack. Women don't deny me. When Gemma rejects me, I'm gutted... but extremely intrigued. She thinks I'm a man who gives up easily. She has no idea that fate has a unique arrangement for us.

This is a novella that introduces the Etched series. All other books after this one will be full-length novels.

www.callazae.com/books

ACKNOWLEDGMENTS

Thank you to Laurie, Anna, Julie and Kaz who helped my story shine. You are the angels in my Heaven. Thank you to my family who always give me everything I need to pursue my dreams. You are my entire Universe.

And thank you, dear readers, you give me a reason to keep writing. Without you, there's no one to appreciate the stardust within my creation. You have my utmost gratitude. Thank you, thank you, thank you.

ABOUT THE AUTHOR
CALLA ZAE

I love writing otherworldly and contemporary romance novels. I'm an artist, and I love to create visuals to convey my stories.

I live in Massachusetts with my husband who keeps me grounded to Earth and two creative children who think I have my own secret planet. They're onto something...

www.ingramcontent.com/pod-product-compliance
Lightning Source LLC
Chambersburg PA
CBHW071804190726
48292CB00008B/2713